chronicles
of a village

A MARGELLOS
WORLD REPUBLIC OF LETTERS BOOK

Yale UNIVERSITY PRESS | NEW HAVEN & LONDON

chronicles
of a village

nguyễn
thanh hiện

*translated from the
vietnamese by
quyên nguyễn-hoàng*

The Margellos World Republic of Letters is dedicated to making literary works from around the globe available in English through translation. It brings to the English-speaking world the work of leading poets, novelists, essayists, philosophers, and playwrights from Europe, Latin America, Africa, Asia, and the Middle East to stimulate international discourse and creative exchange.

First published in Vietnamese as *Những Tin Tức Về Một Ngôi Làng* in 2017. First published in English in Singapore by Penguin Random House SEA in 2022 and in the United States by Yale University Press in 2024.

Yale University Press books may be purchased in quantity for educational, business, or promotional use. For information, please e-mail sales.press@yale.edu (U.S. office) or sales@yaleup.co.uk (U.K. office).

Typeset in Adobe Caslon Pro by MAP Systems, Bengaluru, India. Printed in the United States of America.

Library of Congress Control Number: 2023946331
ISBN 978-0-300-27640-4 (paperback)

A catalogue record for this book is available from the British Library.

10 9 8 7 6 5 4 3 2 1

my birthsoil, hearing the dawn crows of the roosters,
rouses from sleep

In Place of a Preface

ancient fragments of soul are resurging within sleepless perceptions, breathlessly i run through the old months and years to find a little consolation in the words inscribed on fragments of terracotta, cuneiform characters yellowed with emotion, time compressed into shapes, could it be the deposit of a noble death, a hero sacrificed for the homeland in danger, could it be a prophecy of the upheavals of the world uttered by someone who stood by a megalithic structure by the sea and foresaw the human fate, could it be the fury of the god of fertility who saw that human beings had effaced all divine ardour from their mating season, could it be an account of the splendid sensations of awe at the magical beginning of creation, the beginning of the beginning of poetry, breathlessly i run through the prehistoric months and years, rummaging in the soil for the sad and happy sequences of a human life, the traces of survival always making me feel a little less lonely, when contemplating my beloved village i often still see handfuls of old bones in the soil, the road to my village is now raised high, now left to collapse, the houses in my village are now turned into multistory towers, now incinerated by heavenly fires, or are they human fires, the fields in my village are now teeming with rice, now emptied of ploughmen, and yet all these disparate things belong to my beloved land of pebbles and stones, centuries of pebbles and stones have passed, and the eyes have run out of tears to cry

1

it was a morning i will never forget, the morning i opened the door to the sound of them shouting,

'let's together march forward,'

'they always began with the same line,' the social scientists said of the onslaught of the sightless humans

'there's no more time,' i cried to my parents the moment i caught sight of the crowd of sightless humans on the village road

a terrible morning it was

my father, as soon as he awoke, even before he brushed his teeth or rinsed his mouth, was already weaving a muzzle for our cow, meanwhile, out in the shed, my mother was struggling with a horde of freshly born piglets, startled by my strange cry, she rushed into the house, still holding three piglets in her arms

we had heard of the sightless humans and their global offensive before, but no one in my family had ever imagined that they would one day march to our village

'why march to this poor skeleton of a village where sadness always haunts and winds through the country roads?' my father said casually, as though nothing was wrong, 'oh dear, what are we going to do now?' my mother asked

'we do what we've always done,' my father responded

none of the sightless humans entered our house, eventually the atmosphere inside began to calm, but that day, no one in my family herded the cows to the field, no one checked on the newborn piglets in the shed, no one cooked rice, afraid that someone might detect a whiff of smoke rising from our roof, although by the time it got dark, none of us dared to stay indoors

'all must gather at the village communal house,' this was their command, which spread like a holy prophecy through the village in a matter of seconds, the transmission was swift because everyone in the village had already been warned of the cold-blooded carnage that came with the onslaught of the sightless humans

'our sole objective is to march toward a world without navigators,' the laconic commander of the sightless humans spoke, and all the villagers listened to him with utmost attention

'let's together march forward,' added the commander of the sightless humans

'they never forgot to repeat that line,' the social scientists said of the onslaught of the sightless humans

night,

we bolted the doors and lay down quietly in our house, after the communal meeting, each of us seemed to have formulated our own picture of the sightless humans for ourselves, i didn't know what was on my parents' minds, but i, for my part, thought the sightless humans looked just like those heroic wanderers in the medieval tales packed with adventure, so much adventure, and romance

'something's up again,' i worried aloud as i heard running footsteps on the village road 'just a jungle cat chasing a house cat, no matter,' my father said

at daybreak, a surge of curiosity piqued by my father's obscure words in the night made me brave enough to venture out to the main road, i went to the road and saw here the corpses of the followers of the village chief, there the corpse of the village chief himself

'they all look like they were strangled to death,' i told my father

'no matter, son, in my life, things like this happen often,' my father said

not a single gunshot had been heard, but it seemed that the sightless humans had successfully conquered my village

'come on, shout louder, long live the world without navigators'

'come on, take the rifle and march forward with us'

it seemed the villagers had been waiting for commands like these

'let's march forward,' the sightless humans shouted again

'none of the villagers seemed to see, or bothered to see, or had the capacity to see how exactly the world was marching forward, they were quite similar to the sightless humans, in fact, it could be said that the villagers were themselves a breed of sightless humans,' the social scientists said of the sightless humans, with cautious wording

and so it was, that morning, the sightless humans marched to the mountain and forest south of my village, the region known as the Mun Mountain

all the villagers flocked to the mountain to see what was happening, except for my mother who stayed home out of fear, so only my father and i went

'obstruction detected,' the commander of the sightless humans received an emergency alert 'destroy immediately,' and immediately the sightless humans began to knock down the announcement board on which was written the guides and warnings about the Mun Mountain, they used gun barrels, hammers and bare hands too, and yet the announcement board made of steel-reinforced concrete continued to stand upright by the road that led to the Mun Mountain

'may i share an opinion?' my father asked, stepping forward from the crowd of villagers

'the objective of your onslaught, sirs, is as old as faded robes, but the inscriptions on this announcement board are the contemplations of human beings living in a novel world,' my father said, his voice carrying the calm and gravitas of a pebble at the bottom of a forest creek

the sightless humans tied my father down and took him away, it looked like there was a classified command

i cried

'no matter, son, in my life, things like this happen often,' my father said, then he vanished into the Mun Mountain

i didn't know what the sightless humans were going to do to my father, they might kill him, i thought, feeling a terribly sharp ache inside, and when was this onslaught ever going to end?

* * *

Notes on my father:

(one night in March, i went and lay down on the grassy edge of the village fields)
here's the tragic thing about my father, all his life, he was habitually mistaken for an average ploughman by the people of his generation, even by his closest kinsmen, no one in the village knew that my father was a man who carried ploughs and exhaled poetry, a man relentlessly searching for a breakthrough in his own worldview, night, once again, i went and lay down on the grassy edge of the village fields, thinking about my father, the man who opened my eyes to so many things about the world; all his life, he contemplated the world of books, he contemplated the furrows in the soil, he contemplated the life of the villagers, always restlessly trying to build a fateful bond between rice, fabric and poetry, a bond between the soil and the human condition, a bond between the books and the ploughs, most people simply grab a bowl of rice, feeling nothing, sparing not a single thought about where the rice grain came from (perhaps not knowing, or not bothering to wonder what a rice grain is), as if being a human naturally meant having rice to eat, most people simply put on their clothes, feeling nothing, as if being a human on earth naturally meant having clothes to wear, but perhaps it's not fair to blame it all on indifference or apathy, it's true that our stream of thought (an ancestral kind of thought, acquired not without blood and tears over the long course of evolution), which flows within a profound stream of exquisite waters and heavenly scents, often gets interrupted by naive foolishness, this was what my father wished to say to everyone, but he spoke in silence, one night in March, i lay stretched out on the grassy edge of the village fields in the stark silence of the rice aroma, in the stark silence of the night mist, the village was immersed in its usual stream of fragile and aimless (if not hallucinatory) thoughts about rice and fabric matters, quiet and confessional thoughts, one could hear the infants' cries in the buzzing of the insects and the weary lullabies of the adults, all these sounds echoing throughout the village were the confessions of a place ever reluctant to be positioned, ever reluctant to be fixed, all his life, my father was (perhaps excessively) occupied with the task of going beyond the common ways of seeing a place, and suddenly, the place that had been so reluctant to be positioned was transformed into the greatest creation of all creations, 'I walk with the cows on the ancestral land of my beloved village

while under my feet, the quiet soil is still hatching the subterranean sources of life—rice and fabric, joy and hope—and above my head, the sky is still immense, the wind is still blowing, the birds are still soaring, still singing, if people heeded the way I walk behind the cows in the fields, the world would remain peaceful, always . . .' he wished to communicate this to the world by way of spending his life reading his books and walking with the cows in the fields, one night in March, he carried his plough to the fields, glowing like a luminous figure who had simultaneously discovered a way to increase the rice yields and a way to end the gloomy fate that hovered like ghosts over the humble farmers who shouldered their ploughs as if bearing the weight of a cruel destiny, it was a March night lodged in the bright and resonant depths of memory, 'those who have known each other all their lives might wield the sword of doubt at each other, and those who arrived first at the crimson gate might enjoy mocking the new incoming mandarins,' the old verse wafted from the past to my mind, the way my father intoned the refrain had remained intact in my memory, my father was someone who stepped out of the past and entered the studious world of books in two distinct ways: one was his encounter with knowledge, eastern and western, ancient and new, and the other was an insight that illuminated his breakthrough worldview: rice and fabric, compared to scientific and literary masterpieces, were equally endowed with intelligence and power, each seed falling to the ground meant that a new movement, a breakthrough, had begun, the seed would sprout and the bud would grow into a tree, the seeds of rice, corn or soy are all a part of this cycle, as we saw their presence anew, the song of soil would sprout within us, everything was creation's masterpiece, my father wanted to speak of life on earth with the utmost elegance, it seemed to take people a long time to realize that his intellectual journey had propelled my village, a place of desolate birdsongs, a place of desolate lullabies sung by grandmothers at noon, a place of reluctant existence, to finally come into being, one day in late lunar December, as if to wrap up a segment of time gone by, the white cranes gathered over the village fields while my mother, brother and i were shopping for the new year celebration, my father, ever since he was detained in the onslaught of the sightless humans and later released, had become much quieter than before, while the family was busy preparing for the new year, my father helped rearrange the books on our shelf, then went out to the garden with a shovel to clear away the grass and prepare the soil for the planting of cotton seeds, when he went back inside, he told us he was having trouble breathing, then he lay down on his bed, dozed off for several days, and passed away.

2

while some details might be left out, the khuốc bird must at all costs be mentioned in the history of our village, i am currently writing a history of the village, never would my father have imagined that i could write a history of the village, 'there are dreams and fantasies that allow humans to nurture a profound love of life, and one day, son, the birds will return to the Mun Mountain,' my father said to me, his voice brimming with sincerity and confidence, during the days when i used to follow him into the Mun Mountain to learn how to be a forester, there was nothing there yet, except for dreams, on my way to the Mun Mountain i usually passed by a hillside named after some man called Mr Thà before getting to the Ràng stream, the khuốc birds preferred to drink only from Ràng stream, they often perched on the elm groves on either bank, then flew off in search of food and then in the evening flew back to the elm groves, my father would tell me stories about these birds whenever i followed him into the Mun Mountain to learn how to be a forester, my memories seem to be turning into words on the page now, 'but why would the khuốc birds drink only from the Ràng stream and not any other stream,' i kept asking my father this question, 'well, drinking from the Ràng stream makes the birds sing with a voice as pure as the stream water, so that you can hear it everywhere, son,' my father spoke in the manner of a learned ornithologist, 'father, have you ever heard the khuốc birds sing?' 'no, never, i've only heard the story

7

from your grandfather who heard it from your great-grandfather,'
conversations between me and my father often sounded like a
fairy tale . . . hundreds of years ago, the khuốc birds had sung
to my ancestors, my ancestors being the ploughmen in the Hóc
fields who felled trees and picked fruits in the Mun Mountain,
for them, taking a break from the Hóc fields meant going to the
Mun Mountain, they often went to the mountain in the morning
and returned to the village in the afternoon, but sometimes they
would spend the night in the mountain forest, for them the forest
was home, the various movements in the struggle for fabric and
rice oftentimes looked like a fairy tale, my brother and i worked
in the fields and the forest in the same way that my father had
worked in the fields and the forest, this way of being was rooted in
the thoughts of my father and my fellow villagers, i followed my
father to the Hóc fields to learn how to plough, then i followed
him into the Mun Mountain to learn the workings of the forest,
those mornings in the forest were filled with the sound of singing
birds and flowing streams, as it turned out, as a child, i had no idea
that my father was taking me back to the era of hunter-gatherers,
an era shimmering with sunshine and wind, as it turned out, i had
no idea that the birds were a species endowed with a deep love of
life, they sang whenever the sun was out, 'the song of the khuốc
birds is what eases our journey up the Mr Thà hillside, son,' my
father was telling me stories about the khuốc birds again, he told
me a great many things as we sculpted the main body and chisel
of the plough, 'the khuốc birds will one day return, son, and once
the khuốc birds return, every single bird in the Mun Mountain
will be singing all day long,' my father was talking about the khuốc
birds yet again, the migration of the khuốc birds in my father's
thoughts was as misty as the story of prehistoric man's search for
new frontiers, i went to the Mun Mountain and passed the hillside
named after Mr Thà to arrive at the Ràng stream, i went in the fall
so that i could listen to the stirrings of the mountains and forests,
the wilting leaves were a trace of sadness, and the yellowing foliage

a trace of gloom, as the forest shed visions of decay and recovery onto my mind, the fallen leaves were turning into a poetry of the fall, while i was busy pondering the complexity of cyclicality, there must have been others, perhaps many, who were also living on this planet with their dreams, going to the Mun Mountain was my way of following my ancestral legacy of dreams, back in the day, one had nothing but dreams, in the fall, along the Ràng stream, one could hear the crabs and fish brushing against each other in the stream, after thousands of years, these crabs and fish were still living together among the withering weeds of the stream, a cloud passed, or was it a shadow of a bird flying over the stream, or was it a wandering dream of the fish and crabs, who could know, even the rocks, without ever speaking, could be hiding their secret sentiments, suddenly i see something flash through my memory, something languishing and desolate, like a silhouette of a bird, and then a sound begins to stir in my head, a thrilling and irresistible sound, the song of the khuốc birds: Mun forest . . . Mun forest.

3

it was thirty, not forty as commonly believed, thirty people who created that magnificent legend, isn't it magnificent to be able to move mountains and rivers? there is no argument here, only description, one generation passed the description to another generation, who then passed the description to another generation, and so on, as the genealogy of the village kept shifting with the description of each new generation, the body of mountains and rivers became the accumulated thoughts of all the villagers who ever lived there, this is a story about the Upper Forest, thirty people entered the Upper Forest on dates and months not recorded in any official historical record, i am simply following the village genealogy, one day, the elephants, deer, bears and tigers were fighting over the tares and weeds in the Hóc fields, it was an era when soil, water, mountains and rivers were still taking shape, an era recorded not by the common-era dates of the western calendar but by the behaviours of the species, the vast universe was made up of soil, water, plants and animals, whose behaviours and communications generated a rhythm much more poetic than linear chronologies, thirty people entered the Upper Forest while the elephants, deer, bears and tigers were eating the tares and weeds in the Hóc fields, this earthly realm was a realm both non-pluralistic and pluralistic, a realm understood as it was, a diachronic poem, it was from the cradle of humanity in Africa, if that tale were true somehow, that human beings had dispersed to give shape to mountains and rivers, using the same method of those thirty people in the Upper Forest back then, the migration shouldn't be seen as a single historical event, it must instead be observed diachronically by a succession of generations, i am simply transcribing the village genealogy, human beings often encountered each other in this vast life and together decided to go in a certain direction, likely a direction of precarity that hid many breakable calculations and aspirations, it was a fateful wave of migration, the marine vapour of the afternoon condensed with the humans' worries and fears, a life-and-death battle against worries and fears was unfolding with each of their staggering footsteps, in an effort to appear calm and fearless, the humans pretended to speak with the thorns of the mountains and laugh with the venomous air of the forest, they also pretended to speak and laugh with the wild beasts as if they'd known them since the beginning of time: 'hey there, my friends, would you mind making a little space?' one summer morning, the sun was scorching the ground as the elephants, deer, bears and tigers were fighting over the tares and weeds in the Hóc fields, the vagrant brothers came and whispered to the wild beasts, and because the love of one's homeland always fuelled their effort to break open new lands, one early morning in those hard days, the vagrant brothers realized that the forest had receded into the horizon, and the wild beasts had spared the Hóc fields for the growth of rice and legumes, the joyous brothers all joined hands and went to the forest where they danced with the birds, i learnt from reading the village genealogy that my ancestors loved in the fields and kissed in the forest, that we are the descendants of a marvellous love affair, and that the Upper Forest was later renamed Lâm Thượng, a more formal designation also meaning 'upper forest', this is the oldest recorded name of my village.

* * *

Note #1:

The Upper Forest is an extension of the forest in the Mun Mountain, a mountain range south of my village, whose various peaks, mentioned in a number of magnificent fables, included the Chớp Vung (Pan Lid) Mountain, the Mountain of the Reclining Elephant, the Protruding Mountain, the Sinking Mountain and the Mountain of Perennial Loyalty, it was this particular Mountain of Perennial Loyalty that inspired the scholar Nguyễn Cửu Kế, also known by his courtesy name as Nine Segments, to write his famous Record.

Note #2:

Record of the Mountain of Perennial Loyalty

Spring, the first month of the Fire Dragon year, 1856: during my visit to the Mountain of Perennial Loyalty, I got caught up in an unhappy incident. Caressing each other by the Singing Water stream was a loving deer couple, one of which, upon hearing my footsteps, turned around, accidentally tripped and fell off the rocky cliff. Watching the remaining deer gaze at its dead lover in confusion, I felt a piercing pain inside and thought of lady Khang. Even animals, unable to put their feelings into words, could communicate like so, then just imagine the innermost sentiments that could be expressed with the human being's ink brush. Afraid that the recently widowed deer might grow a grudge against myself, I departed in a hurry.

The thạch thiết blooms on the rocks had whitened both banks of the river. I kept thinking of the death of the deer, and lady Khang. The Mountain of Perennial Loyalty was known for its flowers on the rocks, whose perfume never spread in excess. Resting near the flowers, one felt the presence of that invisible substance distilled from rain and sunshine, known as the intangible fragrance of flowers, that put one in a momentary state of calm before the bedlam of the world. According to oral tales, before lady Khang passed away, the blooms on the rocks had not yet materialized. But moved by the teardrops she shed for her lover, the rocks wished to keep her traces on earth, and thus afterwards, a new species of flowers began to grow over the surface of the rocks.

That spring, the flowers on the rocks bloomed later than usual. Still visible among the pure white blooms were several green buds. Although it was already late January, the winter frost from the previous year was still lingering. The water of the Ràng stream was so icy it could cut open one's feet. Back when my father was still alive, I once asked him why the stream was called Ràng. All the previous generations' worth of ploughing experience in my father's bloodstream gave him only a modest power of judgement to answer me in the plainest way: the stream is where all kinds of forest vines and creepers become entangled, therefore people call it the Ràng (Tangle) stream. Creation breeds such fascinating things. The vines that crawl into the stream end up blocking the flow of the fallen leaves, which turn into a fantastic shelter for the nép fish. A while ago, when Vũ Huỳnh, a friend of mine who was a mandarin from the capital, visited Lâm Thượng, my father cooked him a pot of nép fish braised in green onions. After the meal, Huỳnh cried, 'Where in the world does this breed of fish come from, and may I bring some back home?' I said, 'In the royal capital of countless delicacies, wouldn't the appearance of these lowly black fish make your friends laugh at my Lâm Thượng land, brother Vũ?' The skin of the nép fish was remarkably smooth and black for they resided under numerous layers of decayed leaves. They tasted delicious and their flesh was redolent of the forest after a morning sunshower. Huỳnh, after he heard the biography of the nép fish, insisted on visiting the Mountain of Perennial Loyalty. At the Singing Water stream, as I told him the tale of lady Khang who longed for her lover at the hillside called Waiting, he insisted on going even further. But when we crossed the Ràng stream, Huỳnh tripped on some vines, fell over, and broke his ankle, so we had to go home.

This morning, on the way to Heaven's Gate, I also tripped on some vines, but I did not fall over. In Phạm Sư Mạnh's poem about his visit to the Mountain of Buddhist Relics, there was this line, *Từ thị quái kỳ hưu thuyết trước*, meaning 'Let's stop telling bizarre tales about the man with the last name Từ.' I knew that the tale of lady Khang, too, belonged to the ancient millennia and possessed as dreamlike an aura as the exquisite legend of the romance between the earthly man Từ Thức and the goddess Giáng Hương. The forest vines had cut into my feet, which were now bleeding. And yet, I kept thinking about the death of lady Khang. The way to Heaven's Gate was flanked by the Singing Water stream and the mountains. What a thrill it was to walk the mountains and wade the multiple turns of a single stream, which often felt like crossing multiple different streams. The path to Heaven's Gate required one to wade the Singing Water stream five times. Every time I crossed that same body of Singing Water, I learnt yet another new thing about the colossal wonders of creation. My father once said that Heaven's Gate had been around since the opening of the sky and the establishing of the land. As a child, I had thought little of it, but now I was in awe. The simple phrasing of the ploughman somehow encompassed the entire formation of mountains and rivers. This morning I made it to Heaven's Gate where once upon a time, lady Khang lay down. Humans undergo these mysterious moments when suddenly they are able to shed the daily burdensome worries about rice and fabric matters. The forest leaves of January were sharing their vivid colours with the elegant vastness of the universe. The sunrays did not envy one another. The winds were not raising their voices at one another. I listened closely and realized it was not the sound of the vượt birds that I was hearing. It was a girl sitting atop the mountain, her long hair covering her entire back. Upon my arrival, she tilted her head and repeated what she had blurted out earlier, 'Master, is it me you're looking for?' Letting her weep with her head buried in my chest, I kept silent and gazed up at Heaven's Gate, which looked like the lavish royal palaces of kings, then closing my eyes, I decided to stop thinking lest I should lose this magical moment of reverie, which might never return to our defiled earthly realm.

Written by scholar Nguyễn Cửu Kế in the Lâm Thượng village in the eleventh year of the Tự Đức Dynasty, Year of the Earth Horse, numerical year 1858.

* * *

Additional notes on the Mountain of Perennial Loyalty:

Oral stories had it that once upon a time, there was a young woman named Khang who, despite knowing that her husband had died while felling trees in the mountains, insisted on waiting for him on a mountaintop until she died. Thus, this mountain was named Perennial Loyalty. After he wrote *Record of the Mountain of Perennial Loyalty*, Kế sent it to his friend Huýnh who had then been promoted to Second Secretary in the Ministry of Rites. After reading it, Huýnh wrote a letter to Kế:

> Though occupied with hundreds of tasks in the court, I have spared the time to read your work, brother Nguyễn. Recently when Lê Thặng, an education commissioner from Hải Dương, visited to consult me on some local scholarship funds, I read your work to him. After listening to it, Thặng shook his head and declared that this was decadent literature. I did not express my agreement with Thặng then. But now, I am writing to you, brother Nguyễn, to clarify my opinion about your *Record of the Mountain of Perennial Loyalty*. One of your merits, brother Nguyễn, is the fact that although you resigned from the court to reside in a remote rural region, you have sustained your dedication to the literature of our nation. But what has utterly disappointed me is how quickly your scholarly labours have become degenerate. The wise man who follows the Confucian way must spend his life preaching the profound philosophy of the sages to the wider world. You, brother Nguyễn, on the other hand, have written about a man who falls in love with a woman who has been dead a thousand years, which justifies the opinion of the education commissioner from Hải Dương who concluded that your work exemplifies decadent literature.

After reading Huýnh's letter, Kế exclaimed, 'Alas, how the career path in the court has spoiled all these lettered bastards . . .'

4

as to whether or not Lord Nam Hà ever set foot in the land of
the Upper Forest, that question no longer matters, for a story was
born, a beautiful story filled with a gentle enigma that permeated
even the most ossified souls

hearing the footsteps of the foreign travellers, the land of the Upper
Forest roused from sleep, by this time, the land was no longer just
a forest, the đằng trees of the Mun Mountain had been moved to
the alleyways in the village, the khắc birds of the Mun Mountain
had learnt to speak the human tongue; resting under the shade of a
đằng tree, the band of foreign travellers, three in total, all appeared
slightly apprehensive, then there came the sound of dogs barking,
the sound of khắc birds greeting the guests, the sound of gestures
of communication being formed between the strange visitors and
the residents of this desolate village, who could know that these
mundane acts of communication would one day leave a series of
profound meanings on the pages of the future

'you, young maiden of the southern land, khắc bird of the southern
land, you leave behind your footsteps wave upon wave of đằng
flowers, you leave behind your footsteps the marks carved on fallen
leaves, one wonders who was it that came here long ago and carved
these marks on the leaves, these signs of waiting, who could it
be, since my arrival, I've been searching for the Ràng stream, and
there you were, hand-washing your clothes by the Ràng stream,

as đằng flowers drifted in the flow, billowing clouds drifted in the flow, fallen leaves drifted in the flow, but none of those drifting things mattered, for a romance on earth had begun'

the storyteller heard the inner longing of the traveller in the old brocade tunic

the travellers who came from afar turned out to be kinsmen from the north, the master in the old brocade tunic had the elegance of a nobleman, and his two attendants had the eloquence of ambassadorial attachés, these foreign guests were soon regarded by the Upper Forest people as envoys from heaven, they taught the Upper Forest people how to grow rice in the Hóc fields, how to reserve the lowlands for growing rice and the highlands for growing cotton, how to use cotton to hand-weave their clothes, then they taught the boys and men how to build dams in the Ràng stream, they taught the women and girls how to weave fabrics, soon the Upper Forest people began to have bamboo baskets filled with grain and evenings filled with the songs of the weaving girls,

'i, this young maiden, have seen in your eyes my own worries, worries never once spoken, and yet i have seen them reflected in your eyes, in the night whenever i think of you, i could see sudden thunder and lightning erupting in the sky, i could see the haunting echoes of our transient journeys into tender caress, and fire begins to burn me, fire, inside my body there is fire'

the storyteller saw the fire of love setting ablaze the maiden of the Upper Forest

as for the question of who was it, among the nine Nam Hà lords, who gathered the people and established the hamlets in the Upper Forest, and whether that tale is true, none of it matters now, because after centuries of painful wounds, a romance radiating the glint of precious jades was born in the contemplations of my fellow villagers 'whether it is one autumn night, or across a thousand autumn nights, there is no difference, you, young maiden, and i, were like two creatures entwined in the realm of a thousand years,' autumn night, by the Ràng stream, all the constellations could see that the traveller in the old brocade tunic had returned to speak to the Upper Forest people, but the maiden had departed since last autumn, in search of the one who had left her behind with a pure drop of blood, the greatest banishment in the history of banishment, said the storyteller

centuries passed, as ashes, calamities and dynasties decayed into oblivion, my fellow villagers kept waiting for a person to return to the village, believing that generations down the line, a descendant of that misty romance made on clouds and waters will one day return.

5

these are the chronicles of my village, the vessels of remembering and reminiscing, tale upon tale of yesterday, yesteryear, yestercentury or yestermillennia, now plainly precise, now hazily adrift, an abundance, or maybe an overabundance of news that reads like some kind of novel, some kind of novella or some kind of essay reshaped into fictional form, they, the news, the chronicles, constantly expand, contract, compel, pressure, evoke and awaken before culminating in a perhaps inevitable explosion, shattering all the burnished grandiose narratives that so desperately try to conceal the fatal historical disabilities of a land.

6

my village kept waiting for the good news from that greater side of the world, perpetually waiting and waiting, in the morning, when a sliver of dawn clouds passed the eastern sky, the villagers would always notice some strange colour in the clouds, either gold or crimson, those signs of rain or sun frequently made the headlines in the village, draughts and hurricanes, these things could wreak havoc on this small fragment of the world, from the day the land was discovered to the day i learnt to write its chorography, my village remained a small fragment of the world, and yet it carried all of the aspirations ever possessed by mankind, if only one day, we could wake up in the morning without having to worry about rice and fabric matters, in my village, the adults woke up only to resume worrying, a cruel rhythm passed from one generation to another, at dawn, the fathers in the village habitually carried their ploughs to the field, their thoughts filled with the concerns of their ancestors, not the grand tales of moving mountains and filling oceans, but the questions of how many months this basket of rice would last us, or when the cow was due, because whenever the cow gave birth, there would be a shortage of ploughing labour, this small and modest way of living resembled that of the worms, the worms made ends meet in the underground, the ploughmen in my village made ends meet on the ground, i am grateful for the wisdom of the ancient sages who taught me to see the movements of the world, their philosophies on being have the power to

articulate the mournful tears of our earthly realm, but as i write
the chorography of the village, the village ploughmen continue
to remain worm-like, making ends meet on the ground, despite
seeming to be equipped with the knowledge of the contemporary
civilized world, they go on ploughing, day by day, they listen to the
stories of the world, these days it is impossible to pretend to ignore
the daily spread of news across the modern media outlets, my
people seem well-informed about others' stories, but what about
their own stories, the fates and lives determined not so much by
destiny, as is commonly believed, but by severe, tragic and ashen
relations, relations between humans and the land, between humans
and the institutions of the land, between humans and a world
that seems straightforward but turns out to be incomprehensible,
history, like a cruel game, often pauses or slows down in certain
places, my village exemplifies a place where people find themselves
operating in a world that resembles a bizarre game, a world that
becomes easier to notice once it's abstracted and shrunken into
words, in my childhood, the world was made up of what i could
hear in the village, night, my mother again took me out to the
porch to look at the flames in the Mun Mountain where people
burned coal in the night, my world at that point had expanded all
the way to the mountain south of my village, 'that is your father's
fire,' my mother said in a weary voice, but i hardly noticed that
tired note in her tone for i was too eager to listen to my mother's
tales, 'father enters the mountains and turns into fire, doesn't he,
mother?' i spoke like a child tumbling into the thrill of a fairy tale,
although i am in the midst of thinking about the contemporary
stories of my village, suddenly i find myself recalling the old tales
about my father.

7

it seems i have been preparing myself for the moral lessons of history ever since i turned nine, at nine years old, i had never gone to school or learnt the alphabet for i had to help my father herd the cows, in my village, kids of that age all had to herd cows, our career paths always started with the wandering days of a young cowherd whose mind was as blank as an unwritten page, at the time there was a war in my country, but this war, caused by the French colonists, seemed to happen somewhere far away, my village meanwhile remained quite peaceful, we often saw the adults dig these deep shelter tunnels in anticipation of the air attacks of the French, and the older boys often got enlisted, whenever we heard the adults discuss the historical wars of the world, fought by infantrymen and cavalrymen, we thought they sounded just like fairy tales, and we were ecstatic to learn that the cavalry was a unit of troops who fought on horseback, if those men could fight on real horseback, did that mean we could fight on grass horseback, well of course, why not? we initiated our own discussion, and soon all of us, the little cowherds in the village, concluded that we needed to start a cavalry war of our own, a brand new game fashioned out of the ambiguous knowledge that we gleaned from the adults, our horses, braided out of grass, were called grass horses, our innocent passion had turned into an extremely serious deal, whether our battle was successful or not all depended on these grass horses, spring, the độc birds

were sounding their love calls all over the verdant canopy of the
gold persimmon trees, spring was the love season of the độc
birds, we'd begun preparing for the war this spring and planned
to officially launch our battles in the following spring, by which
time the heroic cavalryman was going to be revealed, who would
it be? who among us would become the heroic cavalryman? our
excitement must have rivalled that of the độc birds in their love
season, 'young maiden, come to me, my resounding victory
will one day be known all over our village,' this verse perfectly
captured my state of mind at the time, i dreamed that my grass
horses were going to make me the hero of the war one day, as for
the botanical diversity of my village, mother nature must have
somehow foreseen the day we would make use of the đế grass, a
breed of grass that looked like the tall straight blades of sweet flag
found all over the land, đế grass in particular often grew along the
Tượng river which originated in the Mun Mountain, and it grew
in patches throughout the Mun forest also, we cowherds simply
let the cows graze in the Mun forest while we went looking for
the đế grass to braid our war horses, each of us had our own secret
station where we hid our war horses, none of the adults in the
village could remotely imagine that we were waging a war on such
a remarkable scale, once we'd started to collect đế grass to braid
our horses, we came to regard each other as serious rivals in a
life-and-death struggle, who would it be? to whom would the heroic
cavalryman title belong? these questions were burning me inside,
i was always dreaming of my victory day, my mother, noticing the
delight i seemed to be hiding, kept asking me what was going on,
so i lied and told her that this spring the grass in the Mun forest
was growing very well, and our pair of cows were clearly fattening,
spring, among the patches of đế grass emerged these little flag-like
flowers that had whitened the entire forest, if one stumbled on
these flowers, one was certain to find the đế grass right around
there, we braided the flowers of the grass into the manes and tails
of our horses, these marvellous horses were always on my mind,

i thought of horses while eating, i thought of horses while sleeping, it seemed like the poverty and precarity of our life back then didn't have any influence on us dreamy cowherds, our grand battle was bound to be launched the following spring, the point, of course, was not to fight, how could anyone fight with grass horses after all, but to see which one of us was going to gather the most horses and become the victorious hero in possibly the greatest game of our cowherding life, but the battle of the adults disrupted our game, the war had finally spread to my village, bombs and bullets set hamlets and villages on fire, set fields and forests on fire, many of the young cowherds were killed in the crossfire, while mourning the death of my friends, i found out that the adult war had incinerated all of the grass horses we had carefully hidden in the Mun Mountain.

8

and then those adolescent romances, imagined romances, became my new source of distraction, they began perhaps with the sight of girls my age, we often passed each other walking in the village, no particular intimations were woven into our daily greetings, but my god-given intuition, typical of an adolescent village boy, enabled me to imagine a great flowering dreamscape filled with the lark's beautiful song and our oaths of eternal love under the full moon, 'i will forever be by your side, young maiden,' and like a figure flickering among these sincere sentiments under a hazy sky, i, enveloped in the dreamy fog of dawn, was on a journey with these imagined adolescent romances which often made me pause by the village entrance where i could listen to the love calls of the spotted doves over the bamboo groves and enjoy the fragrance of the mua blooms or the duối flowers, i posted myself by the village entrance where the row of fences carried the millennia-old traces of our ancestral land, i stood there for what felt like a long time in order to think, to contemplate an imagined tomorrow that was as archaic and dust-covered as the lives of my forefathers, but the imagined romances caused me, a teenage village boy, to not notice, or to not bother to notice, or honestly to not know at all about a larger, more cultured life out there, where the humans had found ways to communicate with the past, replaced the gods and composed a new set of laws for the world, where the humans were also holding grudges against one another, grudges no longer similar to those of the primeval, unrefined days, and so, back then, facing the world, i stood there in the same way a little deer might stand before the endless mountains south of my village.

9

all the peng birds seemed to have tired, or died, and the skies above my head were emptied of the centuries' worth of great lives in spectacular flight, i ploughed the fields for ten years, for ten years i walked barefoot with the cows on the field, though not to create a hermitage for myself, in times when even the little fish and crabs in the tiniest streams of the highlands had adapted to the frantic pace of the world, how could there be any places left for the hermits? as it turned out, i learnt many things during those years spent ploughing the fields, i learnt why the so-called 'timely' flowers bloomed so festively, so punctually, every noon all over the village fields, at that very hour, those patches of wild flowers in the fields all hurriedly flaunted their most vibrant colours, a timely bloom was as beautiful and elegant as a nymph living in a well-guarded pavilion, every noon the flowers hurriedly revealed themselves to the world, then they hurriedly withered, it was the hour of illumination and death, i also learnt why at sunset a melancholy blush spread over the vault of sky above my head, as if a farewell scene were about to unfold, it was a farewell to daylight, wasn't it, a moment in time about to happen, although no one knew what exactly was to happen, wasn't it true that the night symbolized the difficulties of a quest? i stood in the middle of the field, in the transitional time between heaven and earth, the freshly broken furrows of the afternoon were dyed the shade of twilight like the skin of a hundred-year-old man, the ploughing cows were about to get off work and go home for a rest, the light of youth glinting in their eyes, i could hardly have articulated my thoughts then, but somehow i understood why i kept feeling a sense of looming loss, i also learnt why, whenever the night was clear, i would start seeing in my imagination the places where the rain and the sunshine lived and ate, i could clearly picture in my imagination the place where the rain came from, and the place where the sunshine came from, perhaps my mother's fairy tales were still haunting her son who learnt to plough the fields while thinking about matters like sun and rain, while i was thinking about these rain and sun matters, a familiar figure all of a sudden dashed through my thoughts: a night heron crying among the dews, well, let's call it my hermitage then, because back in those days, most of the boys my age who lived in other alleyways of the earth were likely sitting in some lecture hall and learning to approach the world in ways entirely different from the lessons of my mother's tales, it must have been creation's playful idea to have the trapdoor snails placed along the creeks south of my village, and to have me placed in a village where, as darkness fell, the night herons cried among the dews.

10

and afterwards, you, young maiden, didn't come around here anymore, the night herons no longer cried among the dews, their cry used to be an expression of delight, or a way of approaching the world, or a stream of honest words uttered as they contemplated their own existence, a struggle for survival of the birds that had lasted millions of years now, at nightfall, the birds kept flying to and fro in the village sky, releasing their cries, slow and infinitely sweet, meanwhile you and i were walking along the village road, our conversations seeming endless, a journey without a destination, until a night heron cried overhead, it was perhaps a night in March, redolent of the fragrant virginal rice, you said to me that you'd been secretly gazing at me for a while now, i said to you that yes, i knew there was a girl in the village who had been secretly gazing at me for a while now, the conversations between you and me were like the conversations of night herons, just a few sparse words released, a village romance in the backwoods was born like the sudden cries of the night herons among the dews, the sound was abrupt yet belonged to an eternity, and afterwards, young maiden, you didn't come around here anymore, at nightfall, the night herons no longer cried among the dews, my fellow villagers went their separate ways, in two distinct directions along the horizon, to tell the truth, no one wanted that to happen, somebody said it was because a venomous wind blew past and entangled everyone's ways of thinking, it was true that my homeland was then tumbling into the sorrowing pages of history, night, the miserable night herons in my village were once again flying to and fro in the sky, not to cry among the dews, that act meant nothing to the birds now, meanwhile the humans were misunderstanding each other, bearing vengeance against each other, preying upon each other, night, the miserable night herons in my village were still flying to and fro in the sky, and they seemed to know that the girl, who had long been gazing at me, was killed in the human bloodbath, night, in the cries of the night herons i seemed to hear a curious deviation of history, night herons crying now sounded like night herons weeping.

11

these are the chronicles of my village, the vessels of remembering and reminiscing, tale upon tale of yesterday, yesteryear, yestercentury or yestermillennia, and i just don't have the energy to arrange them in chronological order because in my memory, the past is a chaotic swarm of motley beings that eat and breathe, and sometimes these creatures entangle my thoughts, making me feel infinitely muddled, if not stone-blind before the world.

12

before my fellow villagers came upon their own doorways to the world, there was this man who had been a sort of worldly doorway for all of us, he had the manner of an aged newsagent whose memories resembled an archive of moth-eaten documents, he was known in the village as Mr Hanh the Fifth, but the French colonists called him Henri Hanh when they recruited him into the Indochinese conscript army during the Second World War, back when the mother country was in trouble and needed help, 'I began my life in that distant land like a flea in the old prison in Mạc-xay,' (that was how he pronounced Marseille), he always began his world stories this way, back then, to me and all the boys my age in the village, he was a truly great man, no one before him had been able to tell such stories, 'thanks to you we kids are able to enter the world,' i said, ' "enter the world my ass", those fifty days were spent drifting at sea, a ploughman tossed onto a ship was like a ball of soil hurled into the ocean,' he described his seasickness to us using many allegories, later on, endowed with more knowledge about the world, i stumbled upon a document about how the peasants of my country were recruited by the French colonists and forced to become worker-soldiers, or conscripts who served in their war by toiling in the factories, after fifty days of drifting at sea, the ship pulled into port in Marseille, the worker-soldiers were thrown into a remodelled prison in Marseille where they waited to be taken to the factories, later on, when France was defeated

by Germany, overthrown in Indochina and turned into a hungry
nation, the worker-soldiers in the factories were taken to the
Camargue where they worked in the paddy fields, the Camargue
was a vast plateau where the coastal lagoons and lakes were often
interrupted by the sand dunes of the lower Rhone river, 'like a
flea in the old prison of Mạc-xay (Marseille), I was taken to Tu-
lu (Toulouse) to make guns, then later to Ca-ma (Camargue) to
plough the fields,' the world that Mr Hanh the Fifth depicted for
us was made up of the mosquitoes, leeches, horses and lavender
blooms in the abandoned fields of the Camargue, the deafening
noise of hammers at the workshop by the Garonne river, where
guns and bullets were manufactured, and Marseille as the city
of heavenly kings who had run out of luck and been forced to
descend to the earthly realm, it seemed that only so much of
those miserable years in a foreign country was retained in his
completely dilapidated memory and, while he often set those tales
in Pháp-lang-sa (France), occasionally he set those same tales on
the other side of the mountain range south of my village, 'you
kids just go past that mountain and you'll see the Ca-ma horses'
(the Camargue horses were once a famed breed in France), this
worker-soldier, who served the French colonists on behalf of my
fellow villagers, was also the first in the village to buy a radio, one
day Mr Hanh the Fifth ordered his children and grandchildren to
sell all their rice, go to town and bring back a transistor radio which
he then put on public display in his house, now that was a gateway
that truly opened my village to the world, back then, everybody
worked hard during the day, and in the evening, all gathered at
Mr Hanh the Fifth's to listen to the transistor radio although most
were able to make out only about two or three percent of what
the radio was transmitting, the truth was, everybody came over to
his place to behold and contemplate the speaking object, which
they regarded as a bizarre wonder of the human world, the name
that my fellow villagers gave to Mr Hanh the Fifth's transistor
radio was 'Mr Ra-đi-ô,' sometimes abridged as 'That Man,' by

then Mr Hanh the Fifth had grown mostly deaf and his memory had long decayed, 'I bought the thing so that folks could see that goddamn faraway country where I had lived in misery,' he told everyone the reason behind his decision to buy the transistor radio, whenever the sun was about to sink behind the mountains, he would turn on the radio and leave it on all evening, one day, a villager came by early to catch the news broadcast: 'ten Pathet Lao army units, having successfully occupied Mương Phanh, were about to enter the Chum fields,' the event had transpired in Laos but the villager misheard the news and thought the Pathet Lao army was about to enter the fields of our village, 'Oh listen up, folks! Mr Ra-đi-ô said the enemy is coming!' the villager ran everywhere, screaming the news, and so the entire village flocked to Mr Hanh the Fifth's, at which point the radio broadcast had already moved on to other news, 'Oh heavens, why is That Man still trying to hide the news from us,' my fellow villagers cried, that night everyone stayed up waiting for the enemy, afterwards, when Mr Hanh the Fifth passed away and his children decided to bury the radio with him, my fellow villagers were once again stone-blind before the world, but they did manage to hear his last words which, like a strange object, kept restlessly turning over and over in their thoughts: 'rơ xuy on nôm mi-xê-ráp' ('je suis un homme miserable,' or 'i am a miserable man').

13

as for Mr Quì, the village headman, he didn't die but softly crumpled in peace, in other words, the dynasty that Mr Quì the headman had served for nearly ten years had finally collapsed, the ruler of the dynasty was murdered, and Mr Quì's title as the village headman was finished, but his body remained intact, in other words, he was still living in his house, he wasn't imprisoned, exiled or vilified, that night, in the winter of the year of the water cat, everyone in my village was asleep in peace, but the next morning, they all woke up to the news that Mr Quì the headman had lost his headman title, i had woken up around midnight, as my right eye had been vehemently twitching, i tried to guess the omen to no avail, but according to ancestral wisdom, i knew it wasn't a good sign, Mr Quì the headman announced the news to the villagers in the morning when all the households equipped with ra-đi-ô's had turned them up at maximal volume, so that the other households without ra-đi-ô's could also hear, and passers-by on the street could also hear, not the news about the battles all over the country, not the news about the racial and religious conflicts in Africa or America, but the news about an overthrown dynasty, at four in the morning, the defence forces at the presidential palace had surrendered to the revolutionary army, said the news reporter on the radio, in our backwoodsy village, the useful daily news had usually been related to things like which new strain of fertilizer was available, or which rice variety was certified as the highest-yield in the world, so upon hearing the news that the regime had collapsed, everybody looked shocked as though they had fallen out of the sky, i also felt like i had fallen out of the sky, the ploughman blood inside my veins must have been so thick that as a twenty-something young man (and a lettered one at that), i barely had an ounce of political prudence in my mind, to me, back then, history appeared disappointing and fabricated somehow, like made-up stories, it was only the day before when i had seen the estate of that dynasty, still peacefully spreading under the bleak winter sky, it had never occurred to me or anyone in our village that the dynasty could ever collapse, although earlier, even the most indifferent folks had probably heard of the internal clashes between the Buddhists and the authority, and heard of other equally devastating disagreements and disputes, but still, to someone without a single political direction like myself, the fact that a superficially stable dynasty had abruptly collapsed was like a wild dream, let's consider this my first time, the revolution in Saigon led by the great generals had compelled me to start paying attention to the remaining days of the life of the village headman, a victim of the overthrow, 'Mr Quì the headman, may i ask if you are upset,' i attempted to ask Mr Quì the headman when i came to visit him as a neighbour, that winter of the year of the water cat should have looked gloomy to a man who woke up to find his hands empty, but no, Mr Quì the headman was still as affable as ever, 'only a little surprised, yes, but not at all upset,' Mr Quì the headman said to me, 'that no-good headman Quì, he got pretty lucky,' my fellow villagers had begun their commentary on the demotion of the village headman, 'as village headman, the guy never even bothered to join the Personalist Labour party, neither did he ask anyone else to join the Personalist Labour party, and neither did he make the young men and women of the village put on the green uniform of the Women's Association or the Republican Youths' (these were the civil society organizations of the recently collapsed dynasty), after seventy years of living through various historical eras, in which for about ten years, when the king was still around, he had served as the village scribe, and for about another ten years, he had served as the village headman under the dynasty that recently collapsed right before his eyes, Mr Quì the headman appeared to have grown calmer than before, 'what's on your mind?' i asked Mr Quì when i paid him a visit on another day, he was casually swinging in a hammock hung in an empty corner of his house, gazing at the happy bulbuls skipping around the edge of a well about five steps away him, 'you know, the bulbuls, similar to you, would also like to ask me what is on my mind,' replied Mr Quì the headman cheerfully, back then, i had so much respect for him, and i knew that even those who held a grudge against the collapsed dynasty never actually held a grudge against Mr Quì the headman, a devoted servant of that dynasty, day in and day out, i kept seeing Mr. Quì the headman lying in the hammock in his empty corner as he silently looked across the village road that intersects his alleyway, could it be possible that he was still keeping watch over the new dynasty which knocked down the dynasty he had laboriously served for nearly ten years?

14

throughout my childhood, my village to me was the world in miniature, and the miserable human species there was made up of my father, my mother and my big brother Lực, this however only became clear later after i acquired a little more knowledge and a capacity for introspection, back then, in the endless days of childhood, everyone and everything around me, my village, my father, my mother and my brother, like some marvellous harmony, all seemed to entwine, humans and lands, humans and humans, without understanding the meaning of everything, i felt happy, life was utterly strange and at the same time, infinitely charming, the fields were delightfully filled with the sound of cows, the sound of humans, the scent of soil, the scent of grass, there were sunshowers that came at unpredictable times and birds that kept soaring to and from the village, it was perhaps my innate happiness that made me think everyone around me was as joyful as i was, even in the hardest of times, when my family had to make do with potatoes and plain porridge for lack of rice, i felt happy still, winter, the rain made travelling terribly difficult, i followed our pregnant cow to the cemetery knoll of the village, and while the cow grazed in the rain, i hunkered down inside my raincoat woven out of mountain palm leaves, in the rain i had made myself a house whose roof was my conical hat, whose walls were my raincoat woven out of mountain palm leaves, sitting on my haunches inside my makeshift house in the rain, i felt like i was enjoying a life in peace, but it wasn't really true, in the hardest and hungriest of times, the raincoats woven out of mountain palm leaves were crucial to my family's livelihood, the world is a set of fortunes, and a fortune occurred in this distant village, try to picture this, back then, in many places on earth, in winter, people went out in automobiles, and if they walked, they would wear raincoats made of waterproof fabrics, but in my village, everyone went out in these raincoats woven out of mountain palm leaves that were like the plumage of an eagle, how i wish i could describe to everyone the fine details of these palm-leaf raincoats, in my village there was a market session every five days, every five days my big brother Lực would carry a batch of palm-leaf raincoats to the town market, which was about ten kilometres from our village, and afterwards, he would come home with plenty of rice, fish and fish sauce, later on, when i was able to help my brother carry the palm-leaf raincoats to the town market, i realized how in winter, my family's livelihood was closely attached to the rain and raincoats woven out of mountain palm leaves, if the rain ceased, my family would also cease to be able to buy rice, long ago, my mother had already summed up our family's winter life: it is a fortune that in this world there existed a land where in winter people still went out in raincoats woven out of mountain palm leaves, throughout the winter, my parents would meticulously hand-weave every single raincoat, to chằm or hand-weave a raincoat, one braided together the large waterproof palm leaves into multiple sheets, these leaves were picked by my big brother Lực in the Mun Mountain, the forested mountain south of the village, on days when he didn't have to go to the town market, he would once again go to the Mun Mountain to collect the leaves, that winter, after every town market session, my big brother Lực always returned home with an untouched batch of palm-leaf raincoats, whereas i was assigned by my father the lighter task of caring for our pregnant cow, despite the rain that day, i managed to get our cow to go to the cemetery knoll, and while the cow was grazing in the rain there, i sat down inside the house fashioned out of my palm-leaf raincoat and wondered why people were no longer buying palm-leaf raincoats from my big brother Lực, how i wish i could describe to everyone the details of this scene where i was sitting snugly inside my house of leaves under the rain, wondering why people were no longer buying my family's palm-leaf raincoats, to this day, as i write the village chorography, this particular object continues to shine in my memory with the same shimmering lustre: the raincoat woven out of mountain palm leaves, suddenly the pregnant cow made a sound that startled me, it was going into labour, lying stretched out on the ground, gasping for air in the rain, that rainy morning, no other kid in the village, except for me, had herded the cows to the cemetery knoll, but before i even had time to cry for help, the pregnant cow had already finished birthing, her calf was already breaking into a run in the rain, now didn't i sacrifice the house fashioned out of my palm-leaf raincoat for the little calf? as soon as the rain let up, i turned my raincoat into a blanket for the calf, i held it in my arms as i ran home, the mother cow trotting behind me, that noon, my family had a bit of steamed cassava for lunch, the cow drank our rice bran water, the calf suckled from its mother, and once again i caught sight of the familiar smiles on the faces of my father, my mother and my big brother Lực, could it be possible that my parents and my brother had somehow arrived at a shore far from all miseries.

15

there was a segment of history that seemed a little strange, if not absolutely bizarre for the era of the flat world, but it was poignant nonetheless, while many places on earth were thriving on commodity production, during this segment of history, my father tilled soil to grow cotton and my mother wove fabrics

one day in June, the cotton plants were bursting open in the garden, it had been more than half a year since the merchant last came to buy our fabric and paid in rice, my mother had promised him that the fabric would be ready by August, it was a promise, a possibility, by June, the cotton blooms had whitened our entire garden, but it remained a possibility, an uncertainty

it's not that i am being nostalgic about the scene of growing and weaving cotton, but it's a segment of history that can't go unmentioned, every five days there was a village market session and i would follow my mother to the village market to sell fabric, 'who is it that has returned to the land of Giã this time,' so went the folk verse, a journey of long miles and bleeding bare feet, when we arrived, the morning session of the village market would always be ready with stalls of fish and shrimp brought there by the nò operators who bought fish on the coast of Giã then resold them in local markets, this village market was a great world in my adolescent mind, i was overjoyed to follow my mother into that great world, and felt nothing could tie me down, in the village market, i saw people who sold rice, sold vegetables, sold fish sauce, saw people who sold eggs, sold meat, sold winnowing baskets, sold panniers, after a short while my mother's bolt of khún fabric had already sold out, the fish and shrimp of the nò operators had also sold out, the rice, legumes, winnowing baskets and panniers all sold out, it was a segment of history in which goods in a village market were simply exchanged among the marketeers, the shrimp-and-fish lady would sell shrimp and fish before bringing some cash over to buy fabric from my mother, and my mother would sell fabric before bringing some cash over to buy eggs and meat from the egg-and-meat lady

one day in June, the cotton bolls were bursting open in the garden, and i was thinking about the task of separating the cotton from its seeds, the world was unfurling in its own way and i was unfurling in mine, thinking about the day the cotton blooms would ripen in the garden, which was also the day when the village girls, around fifteen or sixteen years old, would come over to help my mother remove the seeds and spin the cotton, in my village back then, according to my vague memory, it seemed that only my family grew and spun cotton, it was hard to nourish the cotton plants until the day their blooms were ready to be harvested, not to mention that weaving was a demanding craft, which my mother had learnt from my grandmother, it was a day in June, i was thinking of the nights when i would get to spin cotton with the sixteen-year-old girls, i was reaching that age when romance frequently fluttered in the heart

the way my father, someone who read all sorts of books ancient and new, made a weaving shuttle for my mother, using his little machete, was a declaration to the world that theoretical knowledge could hardly compare to life knowledge, it must have been a genius who invented the loom and shuttle so that humans could weave by hand everything from winnowing baskets to sheets of smooth fabric made from cotton blooms, the way my father wielded his little machete and sculpted a shuttle out of a trunk of wrightia wood, then used the chisel to chip, to carve, to contemplate, to complete the last phase of making a weaving shuttle, was a declaration to everyone that besides reading books, he was capable of working as a carpenter on every single detail of the loom, in short, through and through, my father was a lettered man who ploughed the fields

my mother sat at the loom, trying out the treadle with her feet, i kept dreaming of the moment when our new sheet of fabric, once woven, would be rolled into stark white rolls of khún fabric (khún was the name of the fabric made from cotton blooms), my father asked if the loom was running well, my mother said very well, meanwhile once again i was dreaming of the day i would get to follow my mother to the village market and sell fabric

one day in June, the cotton bolls were still bursting open in the garden when a summer rain, like a catastrophe, came crashing down, the cotton blooms all dropped and dyed the ground a thorough white, my father inside turned silent as he sat watching the rain, my mother also turning silent, that day my whole family stayed up all night

a fine harvest of rice, a nutritional meal . . . perhaps possible, perhaps not, those things, the possibilities, if any, resided within the unspoken sentiments of my parents.

16

the things that belonged to my adolescent years left their indelible marks upon my memory, all through my childhood, a significant question that occupied so much of my mental and physical labour was how to catch sight of the hares and cats of the Chớp Vung Mountain, 'look up at the Chớp Vung Mountain, watch how the cats lie round the two lone hares,' my mother often lullabied me with this line when i was a baby in the cot, my porch was only a stone's throw away from the Chớp Vung Mountain, but young as i was, no matter how many wishes i made, i felt it was impossible for me to get there, and why were there only two hares and not more? i kept wondering about the number of hares in the mountains because back then, in my simple mind, i could only manage to mull over how many hares were mentioned in the lullaby, whereas the question of why the hares would be snuggling with cats and not other animals, like weasels or chevrotains, never occurred to me, but it's true that the lullaby left a deep mark on my inchoate mind, everyday i went to the porch and waited for the hares and cats to emerge from the Chớp Vung Mountain though i hardly ever saw any trace of them, my childhood struggle to grasp the world was tremendously frustrating, time and again i kept returning to the porch, waiting for the hares and cats to appear in the Chớp Vung Mountain, 'look up at the Chớp Vung Mountain, watch how the cats lie round the two lone hares,' summertime, clear sky, broad sunshine, the treetops over the Chớp Vung Mountain were like

sword blades cutting deep into my pain, the pain of not being able
to see the things i desperately wished to see, 'look up at the Chớp
Vung Mountain, watch how the cats lie round the two lone hares,'
there is a profound philosophy of existence concealed behind the
surface of poetry, something even now i haven't fully understood,
wintertime, sheets of rain covered the mountain and forest, sitting
on the porch, i saw heaven and earth switch places in an infinite
transfiguration, one day, probably the most significant day of
my childhood, white clouds gathered in a swirl atop the Chớp
Vung Mountain, and i saw the hares and cats step out from the
white clouds, immediately i went to tell my mother that the hares
and cats in the Chớp Vung Mountain were born out of clouds
in the sky, my mother seemed pleased with my discovery, on
days without the swirling clouds atop the Chớp Vung Mountain,
i never saw any hares or cats, and during those days of cloudless
sky, devoid of hares and cats, which always lasted too long, i was
in unbearable pain, what could i do to see the mountain hares and
cats all the time? i was sighing and wrestling with this question
when, good heavens, a hare, followed by a cat, stepped out from
my breath and climbed up to the mountaintop, on that day of
clear sky and generous sun i saw hares and cats step out from my
own breath, my mother was delighted because this meant that i
would get to see the hares and cats of the Chớp Vung Mountain
all the time now, and then the war spread to our village, my family
and fellow villagers all took shelter in the Chớp Vung Mountain
where my mother was later killed in a bomb raid, now i know it's
just my imagination but whenever i look up at the Chớp Vung
Mountain, i could see my mother walking from the foothills to
the mountaintop where the hares and cats are playing, and i could
never restrain my tears

there is a profound philosophy of existence concealed within
the deepest sentiments of human beings, something even now i
haven't fully understood.

17

there was this shore, i've always liked to call it a shore, right here in the middle of life, i have seen a shore in the ploughmen of my village, a shore like a symbol of grief in one's worldview, one afternoon i went to see brother Bốn Bơn, the ploughmaker in my village, what a struggle it was, but then again, i could see why people found it hard to approve of this proposal of mine, a proposal regarding our heritage, while contemporary civilizations were increasingly saturated with countless cutting-edge tools, i was proposing that we should preserve this cultural heritage which, to those who didn't know the first thing about agriculture, must have seemed laughable, that is, the wooden plough, in the history of agriculture, the transition from puncturing holes in the soil to using the wooden plough was an interruption that changed the face of humanity, it was a groundbreaking invention, an utter breakthrough, no words could sufficiently express the greatness of ancestral thought, the descendants, inspired by the labour and thought of their forebears, have many times in many places turned the wooden plough into a variety of magical symbols throughout the course of evolution, 'Mr Wooden Plough,' for instance, was an extraordinary saint conjured in many agrarian rituals such as spring celebrations, autumn rites or new year feasts, the titles 'Saint Plough' or the 'Supreme Village Saint' were also often featured in fables filled with entrepreneurial lessons, to Dr Quân, the wooden plough in my village was a literary friend (for a while, Dr Quân had formed a literary sub-village with his friends including birds, grasses, flowers and the wooden plough; the poetry of Dr Quân left its mark in a one-hundred-page-long manuscript known as *Entangled Letters*), 'hey, brother wooden plough, do you know how rice germinates from a seed in the soil?' 'of course, i do, it's because everything in the universe longs to change into other forms,' Dr Quân talked to the wooden plough like those Socratic philosophers in ancient Greece, this poetic dialogue was followed by a historical dialogue between the wooden plough and the mechanical plough, the fields of my village had by then been tilled mostly by the wooden ploughs drawn by the cows, only rarely would one spot a mechanical plough, one day, amidst the quiet sluggish steps of the cows ploughing the fields, a mechanical plough suddenly began to speak, it was one of the new industrial ploughs recently acquired by a few households in the village: 'hey brother wooden-plough, so, when are you finally going to surrender the fields to us, huh?' asked the mechanical plough, a provocative inquiry, 'so when, huh?' over the following nights, there were many tossings and turnings in response to the mechanical plough, many circular walks around one's garden or along the edge of the fields, after the breakthrough of the centuries, many people on earth had moved on to see brighter vaster skies, while others had remained close to the realm of the thousand years, how is that so? these enduring questions kept recurring in the region of poetry and philosophy, meanwhile my village had kept smiling to the wooden ploughs, but now i had to visit brother Bốn Bơn, the plough maker in my village, and ask him about the yoke of the plough, a marginal part of the wooden plough, but i discerned within this particular component the existential concern of the cows ploughing the fields, the creatures so close to the humans, one must first pay attention to the plough's chisel, the ploughman used this along with the ploughshare and mouldboard to churn up the soil, in the structure of the wooden plough, the beam of the plough was an enigmatic pole, serving as the bridge between the ploughman and his pulling force, the beam began at the chisel and ended at the yoke that was placed on the shoulders of the cows, trees from the Mun Mountain were transported to my house and transformed into these shoulder poles for the cows to carry in the fields, brother Bốn Bơn showed me how the yoke of the plough worked, as it turned out, he concluded, the cows *hauled* the plough instead of pulling the plough as most people thought they did, they hauled the plough the way humans hauled the rice and the hay in the fields, brother Bốn Bơn's line of thinking led us to a vision of democracy where the cows and the humans were friends in their daily struggles, one afternoon, i went to find brother Bốn Bơn at an hour when most of the ploughmen had stopped working in the fields and returned home, sister Bốn Bơn, who was resting at home in a period of postpartum abstinence, had recently given birth to their fourth child, 'that's quite a crowd, are you sure you could properly take care of them and send them all to school?' i asked, brother Bốn Bơn immediately relied on ancestral knowledge to respond, 'my brother, only with many offspring could one move the mountains and master the seas,' the baby was crying in the abstinence chamber, i peeked inside and saw a fresh cactus hung by the door, 'my wife gave birth in the village clinic, they gave her western medicine, but at home we have her lie next to the hearth, you know, no one here dares to abandon the ancestral customs, well, my brother, i should go coax a calf home now, it's still out in the field,' brother Bốn Bơn said as he strode out to the alleyway, at this hour, all over the village there echoed the cries of pigs and chickens, the sound of parents shouting at their children, the clatter of pots and pans in the kitchen, the cows had returned to their shed, the humans had returned home from the fields, but the unfed chickens in their cage were crying, the unfed children were weeping, the afternoon in my village flowed like blood rushing heartward: the old and the young, wherever they were going, whatever they were doing, at that precise moment they all went home, the events of the afternoon in my village were always messy, yet special, each carrying a unique angle, an edge, a longing, a drowning, those everyday events seemed not at all related to the way the authorities often herded the civilians, folks in my village seemed unaware, or unwilling to be aware, of the political arenas that were spreading in all directions, petty and miserable politics, they seemed to know it was impossible for them as mere countryfolk to follow the rest of the great wide world to that luminous side of polite civilization where one ate like a human, lived like a human and so on, they seemed to know they could simply remain here in this village where the fields spread along the narrow alleyways, and the wind made the banana leaves shrivel in the backyard, and although thousands of years had passed, there were always going to be echoes of humans calling out to each other in the fields, although thousands of years had passed, there were always going to be echoes of calves calling out to each other all through the late afternoon.

18

and yet there were places where people still yearned for the glorious summits of the human spirit, in the long passage of the thousand years, there were still echoes of humans calling out to each other to the fields, there was still the movement of literature along the arduous struggle for fabric and rice, there was the occasional sound of words and meanings, as if that distant land, refusing to let itself sink, were thrashing about, trying to leave behind a couple traces,

for a hundred years, in the hollows of the sandbox trees, the tokay geckos cried and laughed with the changing seasons, at night, the tokay geckos slipped into the shadows a distant melody, sorrowful as the death of crabs and fish in the dry season, teardrops were dancing in the dust, in the drifting hollows of the sandbox trees, at dawn, the tokay geckos gently poured into the morning light a language born of the first sound ever uttered in the primeval chaos of the universe, *tokay* . . . *tokay* . . . there were bewildering creases in the colourlessness and weightlessness of the clouds, like footnotes to the violent collisions born of ignorance, in the disturbed hollows of the sandbox trees, the sound of the tokay geckos made contact with the late afternoon, meanwhile the demons that pretended to speak the human tongue were leaving a series of ashen footsteps on the ground, their monstrous words drifting in the fury of the earth . . .

i'd like to speak of the tokay geckos that lived in the hollows of
the sandbox trees by the village entrance as if i were delivering, on
behalf of my fellow villagers, a note of gratitude to the descendants
of the beastly dinosaurs, those creatures that existed back in
the Triassic days of the Mesozoic Era, if those geckos living in
the hollows of the sandbox trees by the village entrance were the
legitimate descendants of those dinosaurs, evolution might stand
a chance of brightening up, for centuries the gecko families had
been living in the hollows of those sandbox trees by the village
entrance, but once the war began, the trees were all knocked down
by bombs and bullets, there was not a single plant left by the
village entrance, but in the night, one could still hear the sound
of the geckos, 'this century-long exile of the tokay geckos,' once
again i'm speaking of the nomadic journeys of the descendants
of beastly dinosaurs, the tokay geckos used to move from one day
to the next, either taking shelter in the fruit-bearing trees in the
upper hamlet or migrating to the fruit-bearing trees in the lower
hamlet, it was time for the humans and the other creatures in the
universe to get closer to each other, the tokay geckos kept moving
from one garden to another, and another, and another, night, it
seemed that the geckos were deliberately revealing their condition
amidst the changing world,

> all these shifts, these cries, these slips of being, they signalled
> that the true form of things had been revealed, the spoken and
> the cried were the external manifestations of being, the a priori,
> refusing to keep silent forever, had spoken up, at which point
> the streams of blood and tears began to spill, in the night the
> tokay geckos revealed themselves to be a sea of suffering, the a
> posteriori was strewn with sadness and devastation . . .

night, i was contemplating myself and contemplating my fellow
villagers, as one listened to the sound of the tokay geckos, the
careless slips of the descendants of the beastly dinosaurs, one could

almost see the destiny of our village, all of a sudden the night cries of the geckos in my family's pomelo tree began to slightly shift, slightly descend to some unknown depth, buoyant, morose, furious . . . what could these careless slips possibly be, that day i heard the news that something had happened in our village, the village chief had been dethroned, some folks spread the rumour that he'd been making illegal profits from the land of our village, others said he'd ventured to inform against a provincial official who apparently sold off a vast forest south of my village to a horde of foreign merchants who bribed all kinds of kings and manipulated all kinds of lords, lately these merchant-politicians had thoroughly infiltrated my homeland, my birthsoil.

19

it is true that the village where i was born remains an ever thick and impenetrable land inside my heart, 'my village', this dumpy couple of words possesses a singular capacity to rule my thoughts where streams of images and memories keep settling like sediment, where labyrinthine alleyways and gentle mutations constantly form and shift, it was as though they were making contact with some virginal region of eternity, a mere vague shadow of the land flashing in my memory is enough to stir up a chain of grave thoughts about my home village, i am speaking of my love for the place where the placenta and umbilical cord were buried, these things, this love of mine, had gradually sedimented in my memory, waiting for me to speak them into existence, now i am speaking of the row of cotton plants along the alleyway by my house (in my village, back then, almost every house looked out to a row of cotton plants along a little alleyway), the plants used to whiten the dawn light dancing under the June sky, a memorable zone of my childhood was attached to the image of these cotton rows along the alleyway, June, the cotton puffs were flying, filling our garden with a skyful of white, they were cotton puffs, not cotton flowers which birthed cotton bolls, June, when the skin of the cotton bolls had dried and cracked open, an outpour of cotton puffs flew out of the fissures and soared into the sky above my head, those cotton rows along the alleyway by my house had been planted by my ancestors centuries before, back when kings were still in power in my country, the cotton plants reached up into a sky of peace, under the king's command, people from the capital often came to our village in June, the sacks of cotton puffs, carrying the spotless purity of a land, were promptly brought back to the capital, those were the years when my village was known as the place where the cotton in the king's pillows was made, as a child i got to sleep on the same pillows that the king himself slept on, cotton pillows, as i fell asleep with my head on one of these cotton pillows and suckled my mother's breast, i listened to the folk songs that my mother sang, nowadays the cotton pillows lodged somewhere deep in my memory sometimes resurface like a messenger, back then, my country was always haunted by the shadow of the foreign aggressors and i was a nation-salvaging teenager, the entire flock of teenagers in my village were nation-salvaging teenagers, my brother and my sister-in-law were nation-salvaging youths, my parents were nation-salvaging peasants, all the villages were nation-salvaging, the entire nation was nation-salvaging, on moonlit nights, kids my age gathered in our front yard to learn how to sing, my sister-in-law not only sang but demonstrated the dance steps to us kids, those were the magical days of our childhood, 'here comes the red sun, how it brightens the whole world . . .' so went the nation-salvaging anthem (although i no longer recall exactly if it said 'brighten' or 'blind'), we danced and sang in the front yard, in the shade of the cotton plants, and the moonlight was a refuge for our movements which seemed to belong to some epic poem, there echoed in the cool night winds from the land of Giã a stream of ambiguous songs that nonetheless sounded to us kids as familiar and intimate as our mothers' lullabies, but i had to again and again bid farewell to my row of cotton plants along the alleyway, i had to go study the alphabet at the district school (by then i had finished my studies at the village school and my father had thus allowed me to stop herding cattle), i would go home on Saturday in the afternoon and depart again the following Sunday, holding in my hands the silver coins my mother gave me

and wearing a calf's stomach full of rice on my chest, my rice sack
was sewn in the shape of a calf stomach, by then i had flowed out
of mother's womb for more than ten years and yet, every time i had
to leave home, i felt so inconsolably bereft, i wept every Sunday on
my way back to the district school,

> my house looks out to a row of cotton plants along the alleyway,
> every March, the plants yield cotton flowers and cotton bolls,
> and by the month of June of the following year, the dry cotton
> bolls will begin to crack open, blooms of the purest white will
> spill out of the cracks, wave upon wave of white blooms lapping
> the edge of my delight, but i often have to leave them behind
> and go to the district school far from my village, far from my
> mother, i go, as my village and my mother soon vanish behind
> the other villages, the only visible shapes left are the sad imprints
> of the cotton plants in the afternoon sky, i briefly hold on to this
> fading vision of my village where my mother is, to tell the truth,
> i have cried often, for i miss my mother so terribly . . .

my literature schoolteacher praised me for my honest description
of the village, literature happened when one spoke of something
one sincerely loved, he said to our class, then he asked me to read
my essay aloud, this event would turn out to be a literary incident
of the ideological kind, 'you are a fragment of the soil's grieving
soul,' my literature teacher said to me, i didn't understand a word
of what he was saying, but his praise made me feel ecstatic as
though i were flying among fairies, but shortly afterwards, this
literature teacher stopped teaching at my school, a new teacher
came in to teach our literature class, we all wished to know what
had happened to our old teacher, but none of us dared ask, neither
the schoolmaster nor the other teachers ever again mentioned the
teacher who had carved upon my life an exceptional beauty, and
then the bombs and bullets of war thoroughly tilled the soil of my
village, many things, including the row of cotton plants along my

alleyway, were destroyed, one June day, no sight of dry cotton bolls falling in the alleyway, i finally saw my old teacher again, decades had passed before we could reunite, neither of us was able to hold back our tears, 'but why did you leave back then, teacher?' i asked, 'son, back in the day, honouring grief was considered a defective trait, and so, i was denounced for compromising the beauty of the nation-salvaging struggle,' the quiet pain of the wound was still too deep for my teacher to explain in detail why he'd left, 'you mean they called you a misguided teacher and suspended you from teaching,' i said, 'it doesn't matter, son, such is life, sometimes we descend into the darkest delusions, believing we are entering into an epoch of progress and civilization,' my teacher said with an almost cheerful air, i felt history was blessing me with a flood of upheavals within my consciousness, felt like i was a staggering fool in a world of bedlam.

20

life in my village was a harmony of ever-shifting scales, and my
teenage years were an ecstatic segment filled with adolescent
curiosity (brimming with questions like 'why do the night herons
cry so sadly among the dews?' or 'why does the whistle of humans
attract the green snakes?'), what was happening around me always
felt so real, and at the same time almost mythical, my thoughts
were filled to the brim with unending questions and answers,
reality was a stream of unfinished resonances, i heard, saw and
wanted to ask many questions, all kinds of puzzles and surprises
seduced me, 'are all the seeds in the ground going to turn into
fruit-bearing trees?' this question occurred in my mind the moment
my parents started to grow cotton (i'd often heard that rice yielded
food to eat, cotton yielded cloth to wear, as always, these theories
were oversimplified, incomplete, cruel), night, i wake up thinking
about the book of village history that i am writing, some stories
are historicized, some are not and some are hard to categorize as
either historicized or unhistoricized . . . one day, as a young sprout
appeared at daybreak, someone was making an announcement
about a deer serenely drinking water from the creek, meanwhile the
waning moon, wan in the west sky, kept raining primordial smiles
upon these unhistoricized days, meanwhile someone else tried
uprooting the sprout to find a seed still attached to the root, it was
unclear whether we'd made a connection between the trees and
the seeds by then, as those interrupted segments of history stirred

up a series of noble inspirations (science and poetry are indeed the oracular utterances of the subconscious), the story of the sprout seemed to fall into oblivion, these days, humans have discovered ways to produce vast forests (and so here we are, with the sprouts of unhistoricized days, and the forests of historicized days), January, the month when the scent of mango and pomelo flowers wafted by our garden, while my father took the plough and herded our pair of cows to the fields, my mother and i followed behind him, planting the cotton seeds in the furrows my father freshly opened, at the time i didn't know that i was having an unhistoricized state of mind (the state of the mind that belonged to somebody who one day long ago, at dusk, sat down in a cold cave after the hunt, remembering or perhaps not at all remembering the events of the day, the encounters between humans and their prey, the encounters between humans and nature), that day, as i was helping my parents grow cotton, i felt unsettled inside, were we going to have enough garments to wear? were the earthworms going to be capsized in the furrows freshly opened by my father? while my mother and i were planting the cotton seeds in the furrows, the nervous earthworms ran about looking for a new home, but my father had his own method of contemplation, which resembled that of a pedologist, 'this year the fields are filled with earthworms, which must mean a high yield of cotton,' he said, so there was a relation after all, consequential and sustainable, between the fertility of the soil and the life of the earthworms, little did i know then that these ontological questions, hidden somewhere in my consciousness, were kindling in me a noble spirit, an ardent love for the land, i loved the cotton shrubs my parents laboriously worked on day by day, just imagine if human beings and nature were to co-exist, just imagine, night, the one who was speaking wasn't some poetic human endowed with the power of words, it was my father, a caretaker of the cotton blooms who worked on not only the cotton fields but the shuttle also, the foot-treadle loom and the routines of spinning and weaving were the unspoken

thoughts of the cotton grower, his poetry unfurling on the grassy
edge of the fields, that evening, the cotton grower lay down by
the cotton fields, my father and the fields breathed together for
a long time under the night sky, he was home before the roosters
started to crow, on the table there was a bowl of cinnamon tea my
mother had made for him, its froth brightening up a whole corner
of life, humans were entering a new day, unconsciously like the
cotton shrubs in the fields, June, the cotton plants had bloomed
white all over the fields, instead of gladness, it was fear that filled
our chest as the dark clouds were gathering in the sky above the
fields, if it rained now the cotton grower would be empty-handed,
'we were lucky this year to not have any unseasonal rain,' said my
father as soon as all the cotton blooms in the fields had been safely
brought home, a dry smile glinting in his eyes like a lingering
echo from the prehistoric age, while i was busy dreaming about
the day my mother would finish weaving her bolts of khún fabric,
i noticed that a community, unmentioned in any history books,
was gathering in my front yard, the village boys and girls my age
were bringing shuttles to my family's front yard to weave, this flock
of young people, myself included, were excited to gather around
the lamp whose flame was lit by the resin of the dầu rái tree
extracted from the forest south of my village, because there was only
enough light to illuminate the shuttles and some of our faces, the
cave-like activity of this human flock radiated a poetic quality that
all socio-economic matters seemed to lack, the point was simply
to enjoy weaving, along the bamboo fences around my house,
the fireflies, having caught our joyous mood, were contributing
an endless flicker of little flames, the pastoral landscape shared
an evolutionary link with the flames of the fireflies, whose glow
brightened our desolate turmoil, and so a melody of the millennia
continued to float, a pastoral kind of ardent flirtation in the midst
of the weaving and the singing, 'without you i am a lost bird in a
strange forest,' the girl who sang that line would soon be killed in
an air-attack by the French aggressors, but at that moment in the

night, she was sitting right beside me, turning the shuttle as she gently stretched her foot, deftly nudging mine as she stood up, saying she wanted to get some water, i stood up as well and quietly followed her, our friends must have pretended to not hear us as they continued to sing while she and i headed to the banana grove in the backyard, it was late enough in the night for me to seize her hand, but i hurriedly pulled mine back as soon as a late night breeze started to shake the overhanging banana leaves, perhaps the seriousness of the banana grove made it hard for us to have a conversation, 'so, little sister, when will your family start growing cotton again?' 'oh, to tell the truth, i'm not so sure,' eventually we managed to strike up a conversation, though it strictly revolved around cotton-growing, i knew then that she and i hadn't yet learnt to speak the language of true romance, it was merely a cotton romance.

21

and then something, like destiny, began to span over the course of history, dissolving all the great and small blocks of romance alike, there had previously been things like, 'your cows are grazing on the ripe rice of my fields,' or 'your chickens are disturbing the lush cabbage in my garden,' these conflicts, these discordant and opaque feelings between humans (not yet condensed into any intellectual systems or concepts), they were quotidian, like whimsical weather, now rainy, now sunny, these discordant feelings after all belonged to those unwholesome states of mind, those harmless by-products of consciousness, gloomy zones that shouldn't have been present in the flow of human life, but ever since the day when a great new wind blew across the village, there came a fury unlike any of the furies that human beings had acquired throughout the course of evolution, furies that still had the atmosphere of the caves, filled with unconsciousness like the scream of the waterfall in the flood season, no, this rage was not like those ancient furies, it looked as if the great wind blowing across the village had brought with it catalysts that inspired in us an intellectual capacity to associate and analyse, this advent of an intertextual perception, kindled by the great wind, caused my fellow villagers to lose almost all of the innocence characteristic of a people who had once been gentle like soil, everybody began to see things with eyes devoid of tears, crying was now a sign of weakness, they all began to see others as either friend or foe, a blue rhythm surged in the flow of the

thousand years, clear and noiseless, the withered binary kind of
thinking that had previously wreaked havoc on the western world
had now destroyed the glory of a rural humanity, it was a mistake
of the contemporary world to describe this mayhem as a 'new'
wind, there were constant echoes of shouting crowds throughout
the village, this was the contemporary way of showing support
and agreement, it's true that back when that great and supposedly
new wind was just beginning to blow across our village, it truly
gladdened my fellow villagers, they were suddenly able to see,
and hear, brand new things, it was an era of epiphanies, of world
views that seemed like revelations, one needed certain epiphanies
to recognize that one was oppressed and robbed of freedom,
this narrative had been popular all over the globe thousands and
thousands of years before, but only then did the rice and cotton
growers in my village hear of it for the first time, these newly heard
things, like unrhymed biblical lines, held the power to wholly alter
their wretched lives, 'all hail the great wind,' praises for the wind
were spreading all over the village, the eyes of each villager were
fired up as if they were becoming someone else, someone who
could identify the oppressors and the freedom robbers, among the
shouts, like thunder in the middle of spring, fury was turning into
hard vengeance, one woke up to realize they'd been turned into a
traitor by their own compatriots, ways of living and dying under
the great new wind were now established, gone was the former
rhythm of village life, gentle and ancient, all of the rice and cotton
growers had suddenly become the enemies of the village, night,
the sound of the night herons crying among the dews marked a
strange new segment of history, as soon as the turbulent wind had
calmed in the night, the villagers started to hear many cries coming
from both the cemetery knoll and the houses in the village, who
was crying for whom, no one knew.

22

could the pains from the past have acquired a particular shape? after all, the metamorphosis of pain or humans in pain is ultimately the transformation of matter, not the mere stuff of dreams, it was an autumn day in August, an old man came upon the house of this village history writer, 'is anyone home?' i was home when i heard a voice calling at the door, the autumn sky was bursting with dawnlight, a light familiar, silky and caressing, it's impossible to capture the seductive beauty of nature, the dragonflies above me looked mesmerized, as if hypnotized by something irresistible, perhaps autumn was speaking to them, like a vortex in the water, hundreds of thousands of dragonflies in the sky above my front yard were swirling, swooping low, soaring high, in the choreographies of autumn . . . 'ah, it feels just like my childhood,' the old man cried when he saw me, i remember the distinct sight of the old man standing there in my front yard with all his things: a cane, a conical hat on his head, an old worn outfit, a wooden cart filled with firewood logs, i had seen this cart somewhere, ah, it must have been an illustration for a reading exercise in one of those classic textbooks, now which volume was it? i couldn't recall exactly, and also why did he bring firewood to my place . . . 'you know, I still enjoy the way we used to let a dragonfly bite our little navel so that we could fly,' the old man said without looking at me, but i could tell he was speaking to me from the way he laughed, reaching his hand into the sky as if to catch a dragonfly the same way i did

as a child . . . 'hey look, still the same dragonflies,' the old man
said, dragging his cane as he chased after the dragonflies that were
still busy caressing the sunshine in my front yard, the fact that he
casually left a cart full of firewood logs in the middle of my front
yard, and the way he spoke and walked about without hesitation
as if he knew the place like the back of his hand, meant he wasn't
so unfamiliar with my village . . . 'when someone leaves a place and
later returns, upon seeing old scenes, they could develop confusing
feelings, neither happy nor sad, in a human mind the world is often
in this state,' the old man said, i respected his prudent manner of
speech, 'the world is always different in each person's perception,
sir,' i said, attempting to begin an investigation, the fact that a
person pushed a firewood cart into my front yard on an autumn
morning wasn't normal at all, my village was near the mountains
and there was never a shortage of firewood, and yet this person
came here to sell firewood, now why would he sell firewood to the
scribe who records the history of the village, 'sir, do you intend to
bring your firewood to other households in the village,' i asked,
hoping for a clue in my investigation, 'well, why don't we sit down
for a chat,' the old man proposed, meanwhile the dragonflies went
on flying and swerving around the conversation between the old
firewood salesman and the village scribe, up until that moment
i had taken the old man for an actual firewood supplier, 'to tell
you the truth, there is no shortage of firewood in the village, sir,'
i spoke again to invite some more clues, 'those aren't firewood
logs, they belong to old tales now,' the old man replied, he began
to tell me the tales of the firewood cart, and while he was speaking,
he kept brushing his clothes with his hands as if he were covered
in dust, it was then that i realized he was wearing grave clothes,
the garments of the dead, well, so what if he came back from the
dead, i thought to myself, 'human beings could be drowning in
dust, drowning in darkness, and yet they would still believe they're
able to see the world,' the old man said, not forgetting to brush his
shirt, 'life is always filled with the dust of ignorance, sir,' i spoke

to continue the old man's flow of thoughts, 'back in those days there was a great wind that blew across my village and aroused all these perceptions taken for epiphanies, the birds were too sad to sing, I went to tell the villagers that the hostile winds came with catastrophes, but no one listened to me, "down with the lettered ones, down with the saboteurs against humanity," they shouted, cursed and threw me down the world of the dead, after decades of contemplation I have seen the cure for the disease of ignorance, as the village scribe, you must surely know it too,' the old man said as he looked into my eyes, then he stood up, headed out to the alley and blended into the dust, i stood there feeling cold from head to toe, it was the panic of experiencing an earthly eloquence that was utterly anguished and at the same time so poised and delicate, meanwhile the firewood cart had vanished right before my eyes, leaving behind nothing but a fire burning in the early autumn light.

23

ever since humans discovered fire, this element has carried in its body a host of indecipherable tragedies, kindling truths and errors alike, kindling many downfalls also, in my village, the story of a man with the surname of Dương was the kind of chronicle that kindled a ceaseless fire in the minds of future generations, a fire capable of burning down all of the sumptuous citadels along with the didactic theories that hide the vile seeds of the previous dynasties, it burns the mind of not only the well-travelled and the learned but also those who had never touched a single book, in the afternoon, after a workday in the fields, having rested the plough on the porch and reunited with his wife and children over the last meal of the day, one couldn't help but reminisce about the death of a certain man, a prime example of wretched suffering, 'the man with the surname of Dương served the Nguyễn lords as a soldier in the imperial city; after the Tây Sơn rebellion, he disappeared,' this is the most simplified version of the biography of the body lying in the grave on the edge of the village road, a distinctly oral kind of biography, according to a popular tale, these words were once engraved on the gravestone that belonged to the man with the surname of Dương who died mid-journey, although whether this gravestone existed no longer matters, for hundreds of years now, my fellow villagers have continued to believe that the body in the grave belongs to the villager whose surname was Dương, but because the floods throughout the centuries have eroded the village road, nowadays whether his bones still remain there, beneath the edge of the road, is unknown, these days people can only give estimations: his grave is here, right around here, according to the way that the villagers think, the bones of the dead (which exist mostly in the form of thoughts now) have moved with the changes of the village road, this movement from the bodily to the conceptual presented an altogether different way of thinking about human existence, 'the man with the surname of Dương served the Nguyễn lords as a soldier in the imperial city; after the Tây Sơn rebellion, he disappeared,' these lines about the Dương family have remained in the genealogical records of my village, the words 'after the Tây Sơn rebellion, he disappeared,' is proof that the records were made after the collapse of the Tây Sơn dynasty (who would dare to say such a thing when the Tây Sơn dynasty was still in power?), but how did this soldier who had served the Nguyễn lords in the imperial city end up dying in his hometown, my fellow villagers must have spent an awful lot of thought on this mysterious death, perhaps, back when the Nguyễn dynasty had settled in the imperial city of Huế, on a winter night in my village, there was a reader sitting in his house, listening to the rain and wind outside, raindrops rolling off his palm-leaf roof, was it the thunderstorm, the book page, or the night rain that was turning the world into a kind of miniature universe, the reader suddenly found himself wandering the roads, maybe he stopped by a forest brook in the middle of mayhem and noticed how the noise of the fish undulating underwater sounded different than before, or maybe he stopped by a small neighbourhood in the night where a light was still on in someone's house, he entered, heard a debate about a collapsing regime, took a nap out of exhaustion, woke up in the morning to find himself lying on top of a grave, he could see a row of cactus flowers in front of a beautiful palace, whose palace could it be? these humble plants had become a symbol of refinement here (similar to that time when a mandarin spent thousands of American dollars on a mango-pine, a plant once considered wild and often found along rivers and streams, whose leaves were picked by countryfolk to be cooked as vegetables), the palace had once belonged to a military general under the rule of the Nguyễn Lords, but now the palace belonged to a commander-general under the rule of the Trịnh Lords, so this man must have been a soldier for the previous dynasty and now he was a soldier for the new one, the sound of a moon lute was echoing from inside the house, the speaking man was surely wearing the uniform of the Trịnh dynasty, the reader thought to himself, then closed his eyes, trying to forget these chaotic vagaries of time in which vast blue seas turn into mulberry fields, then suddenly hearing the sounds of swords and sabres, he opened his eyes to find his village at war, 'hold on, that's him, the soldier wearing the Trịnh-dynasty uniform,' it was indeed the same man the reader had seen in the capital, 'now he lies dead on the village road, dead at this bloody crossroads of history, both the Nguyễn and the Trịnh lords had turned into the common enemy of the current Tây Sơn dynasty, i see, the man who had lived through two different colours of military uniforms in the capital had finally ended up dead in his homeland because he wasn't wearing the uniform of the latest victors, one returns to the homeland to escape history but it's impossible to escape, i see, i see, now let the thoughts fall away,' the reader told himself as he turned out the lights, lay down and listened to the falling rain.

24

in my village there were sounds that felt regular like rainfall, though not entirely like rainfall, more like someone was drumming a beat in the forest, a beat transmitted from one generation to another, as if there could be no other way, and so, regular like rainfall, the past resembles persistent beings nested in my memory, i still remember how in my village, it often sounded as though someone were drumming a beat in the forest, as for me, i often went to the fields to chase away the birds, right, i went to the fields to chase away the rice-stealing birds, lunar December, the upland rice was ripening, the birds returned, the grey vault of sky kept lowering, lowering, as if the weight of secrets were pressing upon my troubled thoughts, among the ripening rice fields in the lunar month of December, there was me, the birds and the sound of someone drumming a beat in the forest, it was the language of an object birthed on the day human beings saw the links between things, it was the language of the wind chime, which sounded as though someone was drumming a beat in the forest, a sound summoned in the fault-ridden river, summoned as the deer stole from the forest, as the birds stole from the humans, lunar December, the upland rice was ripening, the birds returned, the vault of sky above the fields seemed to forget that it was an era of sharp distinctions, an era of chaotic, lost and dissatisfied beings that kept shuttling among ephemeral borders, a human walked in the middle of the inevitable transformation, carrying both the

immense body of the sky and the little trivialities of individuals
bloated with myopic worldliness, i went to the fields to keep the
birds from stealing the ripening rice of my family, and yet i ended
up mesmerized by them, i kept craning my neck heavenward to see
if i could see the bird in the fable that my mother once told, one
day the bird returned to perch on the edge of the backyard well,
'here comes a guest, here comes a guest!' cried the bird perching
on the edge of the well in my mother's tale, why would a bird call
itself a guest of humans, and why was i out in the fields chasing
away our guests, i'd gone to the fields to chase away the birds and
yet i could hear a wavering within me, all of a sudden the dawn
winds began to blow, and once again the wind chime was vibrating
in the air, which sounded as though someone were drumming a
beat in the forest, the birds swooped down on my family rice field
only to hurriedly soar away, why would the guests of humans steal
from humans, the winds had ceased again, the wind chime was
no longer vibrating and the birds once more swooped down on
my family rice field, only much later, endowed with the humble
capital of bookish knowledge, did i finally contemplate my way
into the rhythm of being, as the wind made the wind chime
vibrate, the birds from the rice fields flew skyward, wayworn after
the journey, these were the dreamlike visions that swirled around
the main pillar of the house of being, or perhaps it should be called
the house of consciousness, or the house of contemplation, all the
same, someone gave the pillar a name, someone deeply aware of
this central pillar inside the house of being, at daybreak, one could
hear the wind as it once again blew over the mountaintop, no,
it was the wind blowing across the village fields that made the
wind chime quiver into the rhythm of someone drumming a beat
in the forest, the birds stole rice, and did not steal rice, as i sat
down on the edge of the rice fields to gaze at the birds, the wind
chime kept ringing in the air, which sounded as though someone
were drumming a beat in the forest, as i hurriedly raised my hand
heavenward with a sweeping wave of the arm, i no longer could

tell whether i was chasing away the birds or waving at the birds, it felt as though there were still a shared link between heaven and earth, all is one, said Parmenides from ancient Greece, and so it seemed that the ripening rice fields, the birds, the wind chime and i, we all took flight from a common passage of birthing.

25

there was a passage of birthing that began not in the woman, the mother or the magical hands of creation, but in my father, this passage of birthing unfolded slowly, for two or maybe three days, to the nine-year-old kid that i was, nothing was more captivating than my father's creative labour, 'son, these are the two feet,' my father said, not until then did i realize that besides tilling soil and felling trees, my father also knew how to make a human form, first it was the two feet, the passage of birthing always commenced with the two feet, a breech birth, as folks often called it, made of not flesh and bones, but straw, one simply arranged the straw into the shape of human feet, then tied it together with a bamboo strip, 'one day i'll do it too,' watching my father tie the bundle of straw into the shape of a human, i kept thinking back on the story of an ancestor who had lived nine generations ago, he was called Mr Thông Thống, my father was his eighth-generation descendant, and i, his ninth-generation descendant, if ancestor Thông Thống could catch all the hidden ghosts in the village, then his ninth-generation descendant should certainly be able to create a human out of straw, i kept seeing my ninth-generation ancestor standing in the front yard, screaming 'none of you shall escape,' as the wind rustled and blew into his magical bag, a cosmic bag, all his life, my ninth-generation ancestor captured ghosts, monsters, rain and wind with a single cosmic bag, he could also cross rivers and floods without a ferry, i kept wanting to cry to my father, 'please, father, please let me do it,' i assumed the descendant of ancestor Thông Thống should be able to do anything, childhood innocence made me feel a little overconfident, i was convinced that my father's aim was to teach me how to make a strawman, that we were going to play a game, but i was mistaken, 'my child, come to the fields with me,' he said to me, the strawman also came along with us to the fields, it was a morning in the lunar month of September, upland rice was ripening, upland rice was the traditional rice in our fields, by then the birds had returned in the sky above the field, an awful lot of birds, in the fields children my age were chasing the birds away, their cries resounding across the fields, perhaps my father was the first person in the village to design this watchman whose duty was to protect our seasonal harvest, once again my father took me by surprise as he drew from his satchel a number of faded garments: a shirt, a pair of pants, a pair of shoes and a hat, none of which i'd noticed he'd brought, once the strawman had finished putting on all these things, i couldn't help crying to myself, 'father, what in the world is this creature,' it was only when my father had fully planted this stranger in our rice field that i realized from now on, the strawman was officially going to replace me as the bird-scarer, and once again i felt a surge of pride in my heart, we truly were the descendants of the ancestor who had once controlled the winds and hurricanes with his howls, during the first few days, the strawman successfully replaced me as the bird-scarer, the birds flew away as soon as they spotted the stranger in the fields, but after a while, things returned to normal, the birds again returned to feed on our rice fields, perhaps they realized it was just a regular strawman, and so i resumed my job as the bird-chaser in the fields, then another event occurred, one early morning, i was eagerly waiting for the birds to come when my father showed up in the field, which i found odd, my father had never joined me on my bird-chasing mission before, 'i'm fine on my own, father, please go home,' i raised my voice a little so

my father could see how self-assured i was, as flock after flock of
birds were beginning to swoop down on our rice fields, i craned
my neck to scream after them while my father quietly waded
toward the strawman, 'time for you to return to the old place,'
he said as he untied all the bamboo knots, letting the strawman
return to his original straw state.

26

the chronicles of my village were always layered with a multitude of meanings, for instance, one day, at high noon, the Mountain of the Reclining Elephant suddenly reached out its arms to wave at my fellow villagers, calling for help, the Mountain of the Reclining Elephant was a part of the Mun Mountain range south of my village, like a folding screen placed in front of one's house, or like one of those sphinxes that watched over ancient Egypt, the Mountain of the Reclining Elephant lay listening to the ancient and contemporary sounds of my village

so mysterious and majestic was this mountain that the French colonists, who had finished invading my country by then and were building an extension of the mandarins' road (road number nineteen) in my village, were terrified when they looked southward and saw a giant stone elephant stationed in the middle of contemporary history, immediately they ordered the local authorities to command my fellow villagers to weave innumerable bamboo wicker baskets so that the modern French colonists, who wanted to resurrect the ancient Chinese colonists' way of using geomantic incantations to control the holy spirit of the soil, could place our wicker baskets, covered in white plaster, on the Reclining Elephant mountaintop

meanwhile, the invisible source and course of life in my village quietly flowed on: the sounds of the loom, the lullabies, the laughter of children, all these sounds, endlessly soaring above the bamboo groves, were the dialogue of the days and nights, wistful yet patient, as the language of the humans interweaved with the language of the farm animals, which had been like brothers to the humans for millions of years, these interlaced utterances generated a marvellous vocabulary that perched on the exquisite colourful robes in my village, there was a popular saying in our Reclining Elephant mountain civilization, 'born into the world, one must know how to make robes, robes to wear when one is alive and working, and robes to wear when one is dead,' (back when i was seven and my paternal grandfather was still alive, i often noticed how his burial robe was placed prominently in the upper middle chamber of our house), there seemed to be a truth about humankind in this philosophy of the burial robe,

night, yet I am still awake, grappling with a lingering obsession of mine which no words could describe, one autumn a long time ago, I climbed to the Reclining Elephant mountaintop where there weren't thick layers of yellow fallen leaves like there was in the village gardens, was this mountain somehow an exceptional place that existed outside the rule of the seasons? I wondered as I stood there watching the wind blow, the trees around me seemed to be tilting and leaning on each other's shoulders, all whispering the same sound, like the breath of a pebble in the stream, suddenly I felt so humbled by these gestures of nature, could the word have truly been there in the beginning, ever since I'd discovered the mysterious magic of words, I'd been trying to describe the gaze of the mountain, which proved an impossible task, and instead, I kept feeling as though the mountain had been watching me, it was the gaze of thousands of miraculous years, I obsessively worried that this gaze would one day vanish from sight, if one day nature were to ignore us, how could we possibly go on living . . .

(an excerpt from Dr Quân's prose collection *Entangled Letters*) nowadays, viewed from my village, the Mountain of the Reclining Elephant looks like a stone elephant robbed of its skin, for the last two decades, every day the ruthless people of this country brought modern machines to the mountain to scrape off its skin and flesh, they put our Mountain of the Reclining Elephant into a technical category: a granite mine, they blocked the sun and barred the wind, disrupting all the soil, water, mountains and rivers that had once been whole, the Mountain of the Reclining Elephant soon ran out of tears to cry

my fellow villagers, having grieved for more than two decades, no longer wonder to whom the damaged mountain is being sold, one day a while ago, at high noon, the whole village was abuzz with news about a sudden outcry for help, as the villagers looked in the direction of the Mountain of the Reclining Elephant, they all saw a hand reaching out from the mountaintop, a blood-soaked hand waving, calling.

* * *

Notes on the Mountain of the Reclining Elephant:

i was following my father to the Mountain of the Reclining Elephant, this is a shard of memory i remember clearly, it was April, later having recaptured this memory shard, i could see the coral bean flowers of April blooming scarlet all over the mountain, noon, my father and i climbed up to the largest rock on the mountaintop

'the sun is a large circle in the sky that paints all kinds of delights and sorrows on earth . . .'

this was what the rock said, my father told me, later, having recaptured this shard of memory, i could see those inscriptions appear on the rock atop the Mountain of the Reclining Elephant, 'but how could a rock speak?' i wondered then, 'when you are thirty, you will be able to hear the rock speak,' my father said and began to talk to the rock, in fact, it was only my father who spoke while the rock listened quietly, later, having recaptured this shard of memory, i could see the conversation emerge in my mind

'who says you can't speak? there was a time when you used to roar, your entire species was roaring, heaven cracked open, earth cracked open, it was an era of change, of blue seas turning into mulberry fields, of rivers and mountains formed among the waves of desolation, that's right, as soon as the humans began to crowd the earth, you fell silent, you began to silently listen to the waves of desolation'

back then, whether rocks could listen or not, i had no idea, i simply listened to my father, who spoke with sincerity, perhaps hoping someone would listen intently to what he had to say, birds were gathering over the rock, dancing about, some wild beasts were howling over on the western side of the mountain

'don't worry, they are just fighting for their share of the prey,' my father said, noticing my nervousness, i assumed he meant that it must have been the tigers or the wolves fighting for the flesh of their prey, then my father took me to the eastern side of the mountain, where people were gathering, there were familiar faces from the village, later, having recaptured this shard of memory, i could clearly see this strange scene unfold in my mind, they were praying or making a sacrifice, 'wandering phantoms of the village, dissolve!' my father cried, then the villagers began to furiously throw stones at a patch of soil in the middle, only then did i realize that my father had taken me to the mountain not to sightsee but to fulfil this task, what the task was, i didn't know, all i knew was that my father and his fellow villagers looked furious, and that my village had undergone a series of eventful days, at my young age, i simply felt terrified, not knowing what was happening, many villagers were being taken prisoner, some said the people from the court had collaborated with the village chief to take these people away, no one knew where they were being taken, the village chief merely said they were guilty, 'may they all be exterminated, all who praised the sun and all who cursed the sun,' my father again kneeled down to pray while the villagers burned their incense sticks and planted them all around, i didn't understand this part at all, then everybody left, but my father and i remained on the mountaintop, after we finished eating our broken rice, my father and i rested in the shade of the minh linh tree by the rock on the mountaintop, we rested on the rock's inscription, i was struggling to fall asleep when i heard my father say, 'finally it all comes down to some hidden force trying to tempt us,' i didn't understand anything he said, but i knew he was dreaming, throughout his entire life my father only did two things, ploughing and reading, he ploughed until he couldn't plough anymore, and read until he died, later on, it was only after i read the diary that my father left me and my brother that i was able to understand this moment in the mountain with my father:

the mountain was a vigorous example of life on earth, one climbs the mountain to hear the many voices of leaves, of birds, of rocks, of streams sinking into the flow of time, of all the forces hidden in the faded and new traces in the mountains, traces, they make us think, the sight of happy birds singing in the trees makes us think of the intactness of the world, 'I have crossed ninety-nine distant lands of temptations to return to the village to see you, young maiden,' watching the tiger seize the cobra and the wolf tear the hare apart in the mountains, I see a repetition of the omnipresent violence spreading all over the earth, it is unclear to me why, at a certain moment, I would either embrace and kiss my lover or strangle the one I hate, that day, I and my son visited the Mountain of the Reclining Elephant, at noon, as we were having a siesta by the rock on the mountaintop, there must have been a tempting force at work, 'I am the daughter of the mountain god,' said the young maiden, beautiful and seductive like the kind of flower that only blooms at midnight, 'I am in love with the one whose words could make spring last a little longer,' continued the maiden, she seemed to see through the tremors of my heart, that I kissed the daughter of the mountain god must also have been ruled by some hidden force of temptation, whether one kisses one's lover, whether one strangles a loathed enemy or whether one harbours a grudge so intense it darkens the sky, it is all ruled by some hidden force of temptation, a force we could never be conscious of, although as it turns out, perhaps it is all within our mind . . .

that year, in the blood-soaked purge of my homeland, everyone who believed in the infinity of the sky was executed by hanging, my big brother Lực was one of the condemned, that year my brother was forty-five years old, and i almost twenty-seven, as i stood there watching my brother's body dangling from the crossbeam made of minh linh timber, i kept thinking back on what my father had written in his diary, feeling as though i were living in the throes of a delirium.

27

if it's true that nature reveals both auspicious signs and catastrophic omens to the humans, then i must write down the history of the hundred birds, hundred not as in the numerical value, but as in the sound of their song, 'hundred birds are hard to seize,' sang the hundred birds in the Mun Mountain, this was a factoid recorded in the ancient folk tale about Mr Cả Lựu, a man who left on horseback in the morning and returned on horseback in the evening, the story belonged to the ancestral life of my village, a village that spread around the Mun Mountain foothills where anything could happen, the descendants, waking up at dawn to hear the hundred birds sing, can't help but wonder about the way languages translate and make the world liquefy, circulating like a flow, when objects speak, the voice and the meaning seem to flow into a stream of sounds and concepts, or it could be said that they flow into silence, or concepts of silence, when stones speak, or when love affairs speak, they are invariably received and retold in multiple directions, the receiver might speak in a different voice, the birdsong is retold in a human way of speaking, 'hundred birds are hard to seize' is a human way of retelling the sound, the meaning might be lost, the mental state of the birds might have completely vanished into the polyphonic and polychromatic zone of the universe, language is the most exquisite and dangerous game of being, and poetry is an infinite conversation where one speaks of the world for eternity, hence the misrecognitions and vengeances, 'hundred birds are hard to seize' is a particular way of speaking in this little corner of the world, my desolate village, lodged in the clouded days and years, beautiful, yet utterly precarious, at daybreak, listening to the hundred birds sing in the Mun Mountain south of the village, one can't help but think of a man called Mr Cả Lựu, who left on horseback in the morning and returned on horseback in the evening, one evening, Mr Cả Lựu didn't return to the village on horseback . . .

> places like Cò Đen, Kẻ Dã and Qui Nhơn are known for horses, horses born in mountain caves, hundreds and thousands of horses, some are two and a half to three thước tall, the locals teach them to haul goods to Phú Yên, it is normal for merchant women to go to the market or travel far on horseback
>
> (an excerpt from *The Miscellaneous Chronicles of the Pacified Frontier* by Lê Quí Đôn, Book VI, on the produce and customs of Thuận Quảng)

perhaps after Mr Đôn was appointed by the Trịnh Lords as the supervising mandarin of the Thuận Quảng region, one day, he was sitting in his office in Phú Xuân, listening to his subordinate's story about the Qui Nhơn Palace (my village, in the era when Mr Đôn was the mandarin of Phú Xuân, belonged to the Qui Nhơn Palace in Thuận Quảng), when he took his brush and wrote *The Miscellaneous Chronicles of the Pacified Frontier*, according to village legends, Mr Cả Lựu's horses were also raised in the hundreds and thousands in the mountain caves, but they weren't meant to haul goods to Phú Yên or to take the women to the market, so perhaps even though a subordinate might have told Mr Đôn about the legend of Mr Cả Lựu in the Qui Nhơn Palace, Mr Đôn certainly never wrote down this detail which would have gotten the Trịnh rule into trouble at the time, the legend went something like this:

the Upper Forest lands suddenly woke up to the loud neighing of horses and the songs of humans, there were horses raised in the hundreds and thousands in the Mun Mountain caves, Mr Cả Lựu often left on horseback in the morning and returned on horseback in the evening, the number of people in the Upper Forest who helped Mr Cả Lựu herd his horses was increasing day by day, 'I tell you what, my brothers, these horses are war horses and we, horse herders, are warriors, my brothers, we shall live to hear more joyous birdsongs one day,' Mr Cả Lựu said, during the day, the horses went grazing in the mountains while the horse herders made bows, at night, the horses slept very little since the humans had to practise archery and simulate attacks on horseback all through the night, on an evening late in the month, under a dark dense sky, Mr Cả Lựu recited a poem called 'Late Moon', then he performed a sword dance for his horse-herding brothers, there was this line in the poem, 'in the cycle of moons and years the moon is hiding when suddenly the sun starts to shine in the arms of the horse herders,' it was midnight when a ruthless mob invaded the Mun Mountain, bloodshed unfolded, all the horses and their herders were killed, Mr Cả Lựu, also murdered in the night, turned into one of the hundred birds

as history receded into the past, many generations of villagers still remembered that figure, Mr Cả Lựu, who left on horseback in the morning and returned on horseback in the evening, every time the old story was retold, the eyes of my fellow villagers would light up once again, the dream of bygone days was intact in their hearts, the ancestors in my village died (in the tens, or even hundreds) for a day of more joyous birdsongs, for a dream unrealized, 'hundred birds are hard to seize,' the birdsong turned sadder and sadder into flashes of regret, regret for the vanished horses, or regret for dreams unrealized . . .

one morning, i heard a slightly different note in the hundred birdsong, for hundreds of years, my fellow villagers had regarded the hundred birdsong as a sort of prophecy that told the fortunes of the village, 'i felt something different, too,' Mr Chửng the Eighth said, i'd felt compelled to visit Mr Chửng the Eighth to consult him, he was the rumoured author of all the oral stories and folk songs about the floating lives in my village, every day the young cowherds in my village sang his songs with their casual 'êh . . . ah . . .' drawl, but never did he admit that he had written these things, 'it seems to me that something consequential has happened, Uncle Eight,' i said, Mr Chửng the Eighth looked at me and said, 'or perhaps there is a breakage somewhere, the birdsong seems to be choking.'

* * *

Notes on Mr Chửng the Eighth:

this morning, a ploughman in the fields was resting against his plough, singing,

> 'eventually the village lands will end up in the mouth of those daytime thieves,' the birds cry from the sky, 'dear friends you'd better buy some brocade tunics to enshroud and bury the sorrows . . .'

immediately the lyric was transmitted all over the village fields, and all the other ploughmen decided to also take a break, rest against their ploughs and sing,

> nowadays the village's guardian saint would also like to be a singer to sing a song about the sorrows of the soil

the whole village today was abuzz with heated discussions among the elders, 'have these ploughmen gone crazy? why are they singing all over the fields?' the elders started a rumour that the ploughmen were possessed by evil spirits, which made me laugh, then i came over to Mr Chửng the Eighth's place, i was no stranger to the way he pretended to be asleep with his upturned moustache whenever he heard my footsteps, 'please stop pretending, dear master,' i raised my voice with confidence, Mr Chửng the Eighth sat up with a sleepy face, 'this time you've made a profound piece of poetry, master, but it sounds quite incoherent, jumbled, i must say,' 'what poetry?' he feigned surprise at my provocation, 'master, have you ever seen anyone on earth bury their grief with brocade tunics?' i was trying to create a provocative atmosphere but ended up sounding rather bitter, 'right, who would bury their grief with brocade tunics?' he continued to feign surprise, 'there's more, how could the village guardian saint, the one who holds the key to the wisdom of our village, ever allow robbers to rob the village soil? and how in the world could a saint turn into a singer? this is all nonsense, pure paradox,' i wanted to upset Uncle Eight, hoping he would give in and admit that he was the author of these songs, which ranged from the prophecies sang on the Reclining Elephant mountainside to the little children's nursery rhymes and the ploughmen's songs, the poetry of

unknown origins had upturned the villagers' world, everyone believed that
only someone like Mr Chửng the Eighth could have created such poetry,
'this is just pure nonsense,' i went on again, but Mr Chửng the Eighth
continued to feign innocence, 'you're right, who would make such poetry,'

> nowadays the village guardian saint would also like to be a singer to
> sing a song about the sorrows of the soil . . .

the lyrics once again echoed from the village fields, 'who could it be, but then
again, what is the point of knowing who wrote this, the point is, one person
singing sets off a whole nation singing, this way, who knows, these people
might actually upturn the whole world,' said Mr Chửng the Eighth, i found
his statement unnerving, could it be that he was trying, in his own way, to
salvage the rivers and mountains of his country?

28

and it was right when my fellow villagers discovered a rice variety that took only three full moons to ripen, the three-moon rice, that the old blind man who played the gourd lute finished writing the song of the full moon (for seventy consistent years, the old blind man in my village had been plucking unoriginal melodies on his gourd lute), he finished it only yesterday when folks in our village announced that they'd discovered a new rice variety, night, 'someone came to sing me the song, this person told me specifically this was the full-moon song,' the old man said, 'or have you yourself, sir, been dreaming and writing it?' i asked, 'oh i can't decipher half a letter, how could i make a whole song,' the old man replied, as he continued to play the instrument, the gourd lute seemed to be making an account of the world, i felt as if i could see in its sound a breeze that was stirring my entire inner world, sedimenting deep in that crooning music was the silt of life along with all the ambitions that have ever been thwarted since the beginning of the journey, all the memories of those that collapsed halfway through the delightful game, who were they? human tragedies had turned into innermost secrets, the old blind man seemed to be blending into the sonorous resonance, unaware that he himself was descending into and becoming one with the woeful echoes, 'it is all the same, whether the moon is full or not,' to my surprise the old man suddenly began to sing, for the first time he had written his own lyrics, it was time for the revelations of nature, or the suppressions from the past, to be unveiled, each human life is a course of changes throughout the century, a place of eternal returns, right, 'you, young maiden, and i, we stand and hide under the moon, not daring to speak aloud,' right, 'our parents also once stood and hid under the moon, also not daring to speak aloud,' the old man continued to sing his improvised song about youth, about the enigmas in a human life, at that moment, to me, the old man was himself an enigma, 'you and i stand and hide under the moon, not daring to speak aloud for fear of being seen by the moon,' to me, at that moment, the old man was a brilliant enigma of life, soon the boys and girls in the village gathered and sang with the old blind man, night, in my village during those days, there was a bucolic, windlike elegance, daytime was reserved for hard labour, and nighttime was for the gourd lute and the floating songs about the wind and moon, wouldn't you call that a windlike elegance? it seemed as though this windlike elegance would last forever, but no, history had its own way of guiding humans, there were many ways of labelling the guidance of history, especially once humans had become resentful, but here i am simply offering a description, history proposed that the boys and girls in my village should leave the bamboo groves for it was time to honour money and wealth, time to praise those who accumulated a superabundance of property, time to honour the individual, never before had the individual been exalted like a celestial being on earth, like the glorified ones on the theatre stage, the glorified ones in the soccer stadium or the glorified ones in the political ring, history acted like a force of gravity that attracted all the boys and girls in my village away from their home, the girls were particularly obsessed with becoming singers, might it be more glorious to be a songstress than to anonymously sing with the old blind man and his gourd lute, since there was no one left to sing with him, the old blind man eventually stopped playing his instrument, and soon afterwards he died of sorrow.

29

in my village, sorrows are like the late afternoon winds, rain or shine, they are always blowing, and soon afterwards, you, young maiden, didn't come around here anymore, i have lived alone with the sorrows that haunt the land of ancestral worry, the centuries have taken pity on this being that was perhaps born by mistake, or by a mean calculation of the fates that toyed with the various ways of human existence, winter, the bird in the bamboo grove might fall to its death and decay into the soil, and perhaps, until the next rainy season causes the bamboo groves to collapse, no one will notice the bird's fall to death, for no creature that feeds on birds would bother to search for a dead bird, and the human species, despite its affection for birds, has only enough time to regrow the groves of bamboo, the plant closely attached to the cycles of plenitude and poverty in my village, and afterwards, you, young maiden, didn't come around here anymore, and as if to mark a process of creation, another bird breed, different from the one that died, is born, during stormy nights they utter their cries of lament, on winter nights in my village, the coucals cry to the rain as though the whole world were ending, and afterwards, you, young maiden, didn't come around here anymore, many revolutions have unfolded in the village, many bird breeds have fallen to their death alongside the fallen humans, and as a reminder of the wicked cycle of existence, the cycle of birth and death, another bird breed is born as the ambassador of cruelty, the owl in my village is the ambassador of cruelty, for thousands of years now my fellow villagers have grown used to the difficult soil offered by the miserly hand of history, even if at midnight the owl were to perch on that sandbox tree by the village entrance and announce that a villager was about to die, the next morning folks would still head to the fields and go on ploughing as usual, and afterwards, you, young maiden, didn't come around here anymore, i have grown used to the sorrows that blow like the late afternoon winds, rain or shine, at nightfall it always sounds as though a gentle frost were in the air, what we call the late afternoon winds turns out to be a thousand desolate years gathered into a single soundlessness.

30

they walked barefoot, my village ancestors, whose robes, let's try to picture this, were made of ramie fibre, thirty ancestors, not forty as commonly believed, went to the Upper Forest, in the old land annals provided to landowners back in the day, it was always called the land of the Ant Forest, my village was in the Ant Forest, perhaps the Upper Forest was the same as the Ant Forest, an extension of the Mun Mountain, Upper Forest: the empire of the ants, thirty, not forty, humans went to the Upper Forest, where the humans battled with wild animals and ants for their share of the land, which means that underneath my village, there are the bones of humans as well as the bones of wild animals and ants, history contains the clearest evidence of death, my village ancestors were ploughmen, the soil of my village was now generous to the humans, now callous to the humans, to plough was to establish a business deal with the soil with no guarantee from the soil, night, there was a man who dreamed that a great sage was about to appear in the village, it was in the middle of a drought, out in the fields rice was dying, at noon, the man went out to sit in the sun and weep, the tears of the human touched the tears of the heavens, and it rained, the business deal with the soil gradually grew less worrisome, hard to tell whether this was a true story or not, later on, these oral stories about the great sage started to spread, for hundreds of years my fellow villagers assumed that it was Mr Thông Thống who made it rain, those were the days when

the scientists hadn't yet managed to manufacture rain, the figure
of the great sage often arose from someone's mind, for hundreds of
years my fellow villagers thought that one of our ancestors, Mr Qui
the Seventh, had the ability to stride across the Mun Mountain
with a single footstep, not to mention communicate with bears
and elephants in the forest, in the end, after their conversations
with Mr Qui the Seventh, the wild animals agreed to yield the
land to the humans, the figure of a good many sages began to
arise in many people's mind, along with abundant feelings of
admiration, human beings began to admire themselves, for
hundreds of years my fellow villagers admired Mr Nine Segments,
in those days, the poetry of Mr Nine Segments felt like a cluster
of small hamlets huddling together as they gently comforted and
silently dispelled each other's fatigue, sorrow and longing, all of
which were scattered among the flowers at the foot of the Mun
Mountain, back then, one of the people who read the poetry of
Mr Nine Segments was Mr Cả Lựu, who spent his whole life
riding horses with his comrades, in pursuit of a new era for the
village, human beings kept dreaming about the great sages, long
ago it was the ploughmen who had dreamed about a marvellous
civilization unfolding at the foot of the Mun Mountain, the
civilization of the Mun Mountain, human beings are always so
passionate about their dreams, history is made of humans who
have fallen down with their dreams.

* * *

Notes on the soil of my village:

(a negotiation with earth)
my father wanted to mould me after his own model: a lettered person
who ploughed the fields, 'but son, first you must learn how to plough,' he
said, at nine years old i followed my father to the field to learn ploughing
through not observation but hands-on practice, at first i simply placed my
hands on the plough handle that my father was steering, and together we
followed the cow

> this is how one follows the rhythm of the earth and sky, leaning on
> the sky and earth to survive, without the earth and sky there would be
> nothing, tilling earth to plant rice is a way of negotiating with earth,
> a way of pleading to earth, please grace us humans with a bit of rice, a
> piece of clothing

my father, a lettered person who ploughed the fields, would go on and on
about the meaning of ploughing, i didn't know what the heck the rhythm of
the earth and sky was, but listening to his teachings, i wanted to cry aloud
that i was walking to the rhythm of the earth and sky, my father and i were
walking with the cows, two ploughing cows yoked together, whenever we
herded them to the foot of the Mun Mountain where they grazed at noon,
the cows usually followed me around or lay down next to me in the shade,
how friendly they were, but the moment we started to plough the fields, they
promptly became very serious as they moved forward, turned right, turned
left, according to my father's command, without turning around even once to
see whether i was still catching up with them, but it made sense, this was how
one followed the rhythm of the earth and sky, at nine years old i'd already
started a negotiation with earth,

> and remember to never let our delusions disturb and distract our will

one January morning, the hundred birds in the Mun Mountain started to
sing earlier than usual, no longer asleep, i woke up to feed some hay to the
cows, washed my face, rinsed my mouth, then went out to sit on the porch,

waiting for the sun, that damn morning, delusions had infiltrated my body, causing me to once again carry the plough to the fields, to tell the truth, i had no idea what the heck these delusions meant, suddenly i felt my legs getting less and less stable, and i collapsed to the ground, as i was trying to lift the plough back on to my shoulders, my father, the lettered person who ploughed the fields, stood there yelling at me, i'd begun the negotiation with earth before i could even lift the plough, a couple of months passed, if someone had taken a picture of me carrying the plough then, it would have looked so comical, to be accurate what i did was help my father haul the plough to the fields, like an ant hauling its loot, saying i hauled the plough is more accurate than saying i 'carried' it, my father tended the cows so i could focus my energy on hauling the plough, by then he was no longer screaming at me for he knew that there weren't any delusions left in me anymore

the month of January stayed with this powerful young man, by this time, i simply had to utter a single command to order my two cows to move forward, then stop, my ancestors, the builders of an agrarian civilization, had created a linguistic system to give orders to the cows, turn left, turn right, move forward, stop, the moment they started wearing the yoke of the plough on their shoulders, the cows were already familiar with this linguistic system, when i cried 'dzọ', immediately my two cows would stop, there was magic hidden in the language of ploughing

one January afternoon, i paused for the cows to rest, the air was permeated with the scent of solarized soil, i lay down in the freshly broken furrows to listen to the birdsong in the sky, i'd learnt by then that the negotiation with earth included the morning task of carrying the plough to the fields without stumbling, the task of accompanying the cows as they tilled the earth into aligned furrows, and the task of lying on the ground to watch the pair of passerines swooping down to the freshly tilled soil, endlessly flitting back and forth as if to form a maze against all the creatures preying on them, it was their sacred moment on earth, the moment of creating a safe nest on the solarized soil where they bred, later, when the humans broke the soil to plant rice, the birds would then take their flock of children back to the vast sky

lying on the solarized soil of January, hazily i understood that the soil was what nurtured both the humans on earth and the birds in the sky silent were the shallow feelings and knowledge of a boy who, despite his incapacity to carry the plough, was endowed with the power to negotiate with earth

and now, i have come to learn that my words, too, are infused with the scent of solarized soil from the village fields.

31

it kept getting sung over and over, although no one knew what the song meant, the song lived through the long months and years, 'look up at the Chớp Vung mountain,' in my village, anyone could simply open their front door and see the Chớp Vung Mountain, to see the mountain one had to look up since the mountain was so much taller than the humans, to look, a relation both physical (between, say, two beings standing close to one another) and spiritual (between humans, rivers and mountains), these intimate relations have given rise to the most profound ideas of the nation, soil, water, mountains and rivers, the Chớp Vung Mountain was a part of the Mun Mountain south of my village, on sunny days, one could open their door and stand beholding the green mountains, but in winter, after the rain, clouds often swirled above the Mun Mountain, and one could open their door and watch how the Chớp Vung Mountain was flooded with clouds, the only thing left visible was the mountaintop that looked like the lid of a saucepan hovering in the woeful sky, hence the name Chớp Vung, our local way of saying 'pan lid', back when i was a young student at the district school, in an assigned writing exercise, an essay describing my mother, i compared the Chớp Vung Mountain to my mother's breasts, and if my people were truly raised on the breast milk of Mother Âu Cơ, the immortal mountain fairy, then Mother Âu Cơ's breasts must have been even greater than the Chớp Vung Mountain, right? 'look up at the Chớp Vung Mountain, watch how the cats lie round the two lone hares,' the lullaby my

mother would sing to me turned into a different space and time
that made one wonder, in my village, the five-year-old children
and the ninety-year-old ladies all knew this familiar and strange
line of the lullaby, waiting for the hares and the cats to appear
in the Chớp Vung Mountain was one of the greatest joys of our
childhood, in the rainy season the entire mountain could be easily
miniaturized in our eyes, it looked identical to a single pan lid
hovering in the distance, suspended in the sky, this was often the
prime moment for us village kids to spot the hares and the cats,
the wild animals of the forest, we would gather into groups on
someone's porch, perhaps sitting there for entire hours, even entire
days, waiting and imagining the wild world that had become one of
our childhood delights, we waited for them to appear throughout
our entire childhood, and those wild animals are still intact in our
imagination now, 'mother, why would two hares lie among the
cats?' back when i was studying at the district school, i was always
asking my mother this question, my mother, like other mothers
in the village, sang lullabies about wild forest animals without
understanding any of the lyrics, i wanted to ask her why the two
hares would so comfortably snuggle with the cats (one species was
utterly shy whereas the other was quite predatory, how could there
be harmony between such opposite personalities?), my mother
must have found it difficult to give an answer, having sung the
words for so long without knowing what they meant, 'two, three
or even four hares could lie among the cats, son,' my mother gave a
cursory answer, i tried singing the new line in my head, 'look up at
the Chớp Vung Mountain, watch how the cats lie round the four
lone hares,' and realized the rhythm did remain unchanged, the
stories about the Chớp Vung Mountain however weren't limited
to only the strange story of hares lying beside cats, the mountain
itself was a reincarnation of faithfulness, a man once went away to
pick the bần bần leaves, an ingredient of the medicine that his wife
needed to take after she gave birth, two years passed, and then three,
then sixty, then seventy years passed, but still he didn't come back,

and still she kept waiting, holding their child in her arms until she
died and turned into the Chớp Vung Mountain (yet another story
of a woman waiting for her husband to return, a familiar trope all
over the earth), the forest and the mountain here have carried this
sense of faithfulness all along, after all, i keep returning to these
intellectual concepts (like harmony and faithfulness) without ever
resolving the question of that mysterious line of the lullaby, why
didn't we see other things when we looked up at the mountaintop,
like green canopies for example, or a white frothy stream, or clouds
swirling atop the mountain on rainy days . . . like my mother, i
found it difficult to understand until i stumbled on what Dr Quân
had written in his prose collection *Entangled Letters*:

('and then I started to blurt out nonsensical words')
and then, like many others in the village, I felt my insides entirely
crushed, that damn crossroads of history, I saw myself falling into
a miserable battlefield, inescapable dreams, it was like what I read
in ancient novels, wasn't it? my familiar village was now turned
into a battlefield filled with the sound of gunshots and the false
silence of hidden strategies, two regimes, no, three regimes, three
regimes to be precise, declining, collapsing or thriving, there
were three dynasties in total at the time, all three seemed to see
around themselves an aura of sunrise, all thought themselves to be
a dawn filled with aromatic flowers and exotic grasses, their ego
carried an aura of death, in fact, by then, the long night of history
had draped the earth, hence what happened in my village, but
who could tell what the truth really was, back then, no one could
tell what the truth was, there were those who crossed the Linh
Giang river, spreading official exhortations, calling everyone else
invaders, there were also those who came from Tây Sơn, the
forested mountain of noble disciplines, and labelled everyone
else the common enemy of the people, and there were those who
roamed the south and called everyone else traitors, night, I lay
down to listen to the barking dogs all over the village and the

hurried footsteps along my alleyway, feeling like I was about to be taken away, not sure where, but I kept feeling like I was about to be taken to a deep hidden alley, back then, history was like a series of dark alleys, gloomy and dusty, fear constantly haunted my thoughts, fear of falling down in a place devoid of human laughter, one night, late spring, the trees in the village were trying to hold on to their youthful greenness, night had barely fallen when the village dogs began to bark like mad, they sounded as though a pack of people had entered the village and were about to kill them all, it made sense that the dogs were afraid, strangers who wanted to take someone away from the village must usually kill their dogs first, this time, it seemed all of the village dogs were barking, their roaring barks crushed my insides as if someone were hacking my body into pieces with a knife, morning, I assumed that many young men in the village had been taken away, just like the previous times, but no, only Mr Thời the village chief went missing, the villagers quietly went to look for him, but neither he nor his corpse was found, the wife and kids of Mr Thời the village chief shut their doors and wept, back in the day, one couldn't just cry or laugh when one wanted to cry or laugh, the wife and kids of the village chief kept waiting, the entire village kept waiting, one month, two months, then six, then seven months, and still no news of him at all, one day a villager discovered on the slope of the Chớp Vung Mountain a decayed corpse, from his beard and the village seal tied to his belt, people were able to tell that it was Mr Thời the village chief, but no one dared say a word about why the village chief was dead, was it because he was afraid, tried to escape and died in the mountains? or did they capture him, kill him and abandon his body in the mountains? the villagers quietly carried the village chief's corpse back to his house to be coffined, I came over to visit, looked at the body, tried to hold back my tears, these days human lives had become so insignificant, suddenly I looked up at the Chớp Vung Mountain and noticed how the cats were lying around two lone hares.

* * *

Note:

the above passage is an excerpt from the prose collection *Entangled Letters* by Dr Quân, i was the one who gave the collection its title, this prose collection was likely composed in the late eighteenth century, someone must have read the writings of Dr Quân, and so that final line, originally a six-eight couplet, was orally transmitted beyond the walls of the court and transformed into a folk lullaby, 'look up at the Chớp Vung Mountain, watch how the cats lie round the two lone hares.'

32

i went to the Mun Mountain once again, how many times had i gone to the Mun Mountain now? i can no longer remember, it was all but a dream, there was a change in the voices of the mountain birds, no more sorrowful tones urging the desolate clouds to hurry up and return to the north where grey echoes were bred, their melodic songs were a little hastier, a little more dramatic, and at the same time they were a condensation of a thousand-year-long gathering, the birdsongs gathered the vital spirit of a species that took refuge in the vast sky

draping this tale are the curses that have dissolved into dust, enveloping the deepest niches of memory, although it is hard to tell who was doing the cursing and who was being cursed, this is the whitish kind of memory, like an unconscious poetry, always emerging when one feels the most exquisite agony, and there is no need to mention the name of this and that dynasty, or the name of this and that king, for all sinful dynasties and all sinful kings belong to the same category,

brush off the moss on the rocks where you'll find the traces

it is commonly said that one went to the Hazel Water pagoda, but to be more precise, i went to the Hazel Water stream in the Mun Mountain where the ruins of a pagoda from previous centuries lay

along the stream, and only fools like me would take the time to go
search for something like this, the thing for which i was searching
was a brittle concept that people often dredged up from the flow of
history only to later proclaim that this wasn't it, the Mun Mountain
and the Hazel Water stream were counted among my country's
lowest-ranked mountains and rivers, which meant that if i didn't
speak of them, no one would have heard of them, except for the
ploughmen working in the foothills, one hot sunny morning, the
coalmen and loggers of my village went to the Mun Mountain and
discovered a pagoda by the rocky stream, the pagoda's roof was
made of cogon grass and its walls palm leaves, a young abbot asked
his only follower, a beautiful nun, to welcome the foresters into
the pagoda and invite them to listen to the sutras, that was how
the story went, for hundreds of years it has begun the same way

brush off the moss on the rocks where you'll find the traces

i sat down by the Hazel Water stream, although it was already
summertime, the stream water was still running, i tried to search
in the glittering water for the traces of a person who broke loose
from a manhunt in the night, a hunt orchestrated by a ravaged
dynasty engulfed in the power struggles for the throne, 'Mun
Mountain . . . Mun Mountain,' in the silence of history one could
sense only the whispers of the land, the traces of a tale passed
down from generation to generation: 'as soon as Nguyễn Phúc
Lan, the second son of Lord Nguyễn Phúc Nguyên (1613–35),
was enthroned, he immediately ordered a purge of all the allies of
his sibling, Nguyễn Phúc Anh, but missed one young mandarin
who worked for Anh and was the lover of princess Ngọc Khoa, the
third daughter of the lord . . .' (their survival in that bloody purge
later led to a monkhood, a romance and yet another bloody purge)

brush off the moss on the rocks where you'll find that brittle
concept people often dredged up from the flow of history

only to later proclaim that this wasn't it: the concept of a dark
segment of history

people were hoping that the abbot at the Hazel Water pagoda,
or the man who had survived the purge in the capital, known as
the monk Minh Từ, and the beautiful nun, who had once been
princess Ngọc Khoa, would one day give birth to a baby monk,
but no, it never happened, the land by the Hazel Water stream
yielded all kinds of fruits and vegetables to be traded for rice at
the pagoda, at night, people in the Upper Forest could hear the
sound of chanted sutras reverberating down from the mountains,
everyone assumed that the land of the Buddha must be a place
of peace, where the teacher Minh Từ and his disciple chanted
sutras and tilled the soil to plant vegetables, in the iciness of
the winter night air, sharp enough to pierce the bones, Ngọc
Khoa spread her hair on the ground to make a warm blanket for
Từ, one scorching noon under the summer sun, Từ and Ngọc
Khoa lay down next to each other in the rocky stream of the
forest, where they sent the force of eternity into each other's
flesh, wouldn't the Buddha be glad to witness this spectacular
romance in the middle of our worldly realm, the mountains
didn't breathe a word, the forest birds didn't breathe a word, the
people of the Upper Forest didn't breathe a word, how could the
act of concealing the exiled be considered a violation against
the heavenly law, the months and years never wore away the
magic of this tale, they simply saw the shade of youth in the hair
of Từ and Ngọc Khoa gradually fade

'Mun Mountain, Mun Mountain . . .' the mountain range closely
attached to the history of my village, i want to speak honestly of
it, forever, so that i will no longer have to keep thinking about it
in misery, for the mountains, like pictures, or silent secret words,
contain an overabundance of parables, tales compressed beneath
the endless years and months, compressed and resounding, this

small place in the universe, once touched, resounds with a stream
of occult words and senses

   brush off the moss on the rocks where you'll find the traces

one morning, under the shining sun, the foresters all headed to
the Mun Mountain to witness the scene of prosecution in the
Hazel Water pagoda, where the abbot and the nun were tied down
next to each other in the front yard, when the commander of the
imperial soldiers yelled 'behead!' their two severed heads fell down
at the exact same time, for hundreds of years now, that's been how
the story goes

perhaps, the mountain itself was a secret mantra.

33

in the case of Mr Hoành (full name: Lê Hoành, a tenth-generation
descendant of Dr Lê Quân), there weren't any mantras, but quite
a few maxims, 'wine enters into me, sky and earth enter into me,'
Mr Hoành often said, those were his maxims on wine, as the
scribe who records the village history, i'm using the word maxim
to signal the importance of this sociological event although there
is no actual system of thought or philosophy here, maxim is only
a word selected by this village scribe to gently exaggerate the
importance, and elegance, of this desolate village, the significance
of the story doesn't originate in the language but in the life of
Mr Hoành himself, a top graduate in literary studies, who later
worked as a translator for the American army during the war,
then got arrested by his countrymen, afterwards got released by
his countrymen and was eventually allowed to go home, where he
ploughed his fields and raised his goats (ploughing the fields for
rice and raising the goats for milk), 'is this old fella trying to resist
the globalization of our flat world or something?' several scholars
in the capital said so about Mr Hoành when they heard his story,
at seventy years old, Mr Hoành suddenly found himself anchored
by his own philosophy of wine: 'wine enters into me, sky and earth
enter into me,' the man who had roamed the earth, imbibed all
kinds of European and American wine, read all kinds of literary
and philosophical books, one day discovered the path of wine, a
full-circle journey, like the circular philosophy of alluvium in the

Indo-Gangetic plains, the humans grew rice, then distilled rice into wine, then wine returned to dwell in the humans, this cycle that ran from humans to rice plant to rice grain to wine and finally back to humans, it was a theory invented and practised by Mr Hoành himself, 'but sir, why does rice have to be brewed until late in the year before getting distilled?' i asked him, back then, in the village, everyone addressed him as sir, and Mr Hoành seemed to secretly enjoy being addressed as a sir, 'the rice grain carried within itself the voice of heaven and earth, which becomes even clearer when brewed between heaven and earth for one whole year,' Mr Hoành explained, that was the first conversation on wine between me and Mr Hoành, all these years, at the foot of the Mun Mountain, in my village, these silent events unfolded like the rare gusts of breeze passing through the humid heat of the world and the fatal pressure of our own preoccupations with rice and fabric matters, and yet there was a brief period of serenity, lasting just one day or two, when delightful conversations and laughter filled the air, 'wine enters into me, sky and earth enter into me,' an encounter, spectacular and harmonious, between humans and the realm of heaven and earth was unfurling in this outpouring, a singular moment on earth: the celebration day of Mr Hoành's wine, his process of making wine always began like this, with a few handfuls of paddy harvested and milled by Mr Hoành himself, then the rice would be fermented from December the seventh of the previous year to December the seventh of the following year (by the lunar calendar), at which point the rice would be distilled into wine, 'the wine of this Mr Hoành has all the poetic tastes of the seasons, to drink the wine of this Mr Hoành is to jump into the pool of seasonal movements,' so went the speech of Mr Hoành on the day we celebrated his wine, every year, on lunar December the seventh, the whole village gathered at his place to drink wine with him, wine distilled by Mr Hoành himself, wine served as it was distilled, still warm, none of the guests was allowed to go home before all the wine was gone, back then, in my village, except for the little children, everybody got drunk, including the elders whose lives were on the verge of evaporating, they remained drunk until the following morning, which meant that the ploughing and farming all had to be paused, everything was paused, so that everybody could experience this brief moment of peace in a life filled with precarity, to drink wine once a year, to get drunk and feel peace for once, that was the core of Mr Hoành's philosophy of wine, if it could be called a philosophy at all, but whether it ushered in a new civilization at the foot of the Mun Mountain, well, i wouldn't know the answer.

* * *

Note: a flash interview i conducted with Mr Hoành
(tentatively titled 'something is turning')

'sir, just to refresh everyone's memory, could you please provide a brief summary of your life so far?'

'born at the foot of the Mun Mountain, close to the venomous wind of the mountain forests, day by day lay in the cot, got breastfed by mother, heard the tigers roar in the mountains, ate rice, drank water, grew up, walked around the village, ploughed fields, herded cows, later on, ate letters, exited the village, walked around the earth, got fed up, returned home, by which point the village had gotten older than before, got saddened, began to make wine for myself, to drink.'

'and those days of walking around the earth, could you summarize what you saw?'

'many things, but in short, saw humans walking in the streets, huge crowds, sometimes they paused to cry, then walked on, sometimes they paused again to laugh, or dance, or sing, or scream, sometimes they paused to praise each other, or curse each other, or shoot and kill each other . . . in short, I felt everyone was lost.'

'is that all?'

'that is all.'

'but sir, do you think you are lost?'

'not at all, for I have returned to my birthplace.'

'could you speak in simpler terms, please?'

'if I can still remember the way back to the place where I crawled out of my mother onto earth, that means the primeval image still remains intact in my consciousness.'

'and so, those who never get lost are those who never forget what shaped their primeval form?'

'one can put it that way, but that's a little too quiet, too passive, let's add a little flavour, we could never lose ourselves, as in we could never let ourselves turn into inert things, because in our consciousness, something is turning.'

34

and now, it's time for the story of the letter-eaters, extracted from the prose collection *Entangled Letters* of Dr Quân:

they stuffed themselves with the letters of the alphabet and released all kinds of things from their mouth, I saw them first releasing flowers and butterflies fluttering above the pavilions, the chambers, the towers, the palaces, they always left their house in a stream of chariots, in the afternoon, the sound of their neighing horses reverberated all over the festival where all kinds of country belles and beauty queens were moving about like flowers floating in water, but no matter where they went, they always remembered to return to their dwelling place, a great and thrilling burrow, seen from a contemporary perspective, the letters entered their belly and turned them into flowers and butterflies hovering above the skin and hair of exquisite maidens, the letters entered their belly and made their bodies gentler, their voices and laughs softer, so that they could enjoy the pleasures of life while others mistakenly believed that those bodies, voices and laughs belonged to a genuinely sophisticated people, and it was true that as the letters entered them, the coins they made in filthy alleyways immediately turned into apparently valuable coins (for their proclaimed origins were always global, the money was invariably flowing from world banks, transnational banks and so on, these words are my addition), in other words,

without metaphors, these filthy coins, once touched by the
magic of letters, turned into heavenly dwellings on earth,
and it was true that standing in these crowded, impoverished
places, standing in these ghetto slums, under these makeshift
roofs beneath the bridge, amidst these endless movements in
the sun and rain, one could be unnerved and dazed, absolutely
unnerved and dazed, by the magic of these saints (who went
by many novel names, like Cô-pô-ra-tion, or Corporation, or
Group, all the same thing, again these words are my own
addition), day and night they used florid, extravagant, brocade-
like letters to arouse and invite everyone to come to them and
seek happiness, after stuffing themselves with letters, besides
releasing flowers and butterflies, they also released the formulas
for manufacturing food, letters and food, and then they also
used letters to mobilize animals, even plants, even minerals,
calling all creatures, even mud, even soil, to collaborate with
them in their gated territory, a thousand-year-long course of
overwhelming movements, like the overwhelming movements
of the saints that once created sustenance for the humans, day
and night, intoxicated with desires for appearance and wealth,
they'd totally forgotten that humans ate differently from beasts,
oh, these times when letters could manufacture food, these
times when humans ingested letters, and then, having stuffed
themselves with letters, besides releasing flowers, butterflies and
food, they went on to release many other attractive products,
products that looked like clouds with five different shades in the
spring sky at dawn, when birds sang in the pervasive perfume of
soil, no, it was even more enticing, for these were the products
for humans to consume and feel as though they were flying to
the highest realm . . . soaring superior and noble to the realm
of happiness, the realm of freedom, the realm of 'new life'
(a term coined by the poet Tản Đà from previous centuries—
my note), after eating their products, humans were to leave
behind all their miseries and sufferings, 'all hail the letters,' the

horde of people that manufactured happiness and freedom were always praising the letters and manipulating their meanings, having stuffed themselves with letters, besides releasing flowers, butterflies, food, happiness and freedom, they also revealed the formulas for manufacturing trash, using the materials that have been discarded by the world, like poetry and prose that praised the most ruthless emperors and lords, false records of history, theories that brought about mass death for the human race, I saw their lips curve upward to finely rephrase what had long been considered garbage into some novel-sounding lines, oh, these times of humans manufacturing new letters out of old letters, these times of humans manufacturing letters out of garbage, I met with someone who ate letters once, it was my childhood friend whom I will never forgive, not even on my deathbed, one summer day in the capital, courtiers on horseback were leisurely heading to their morning meeting, I had travelled from the village and arrived in the capital to visit my childhood friend who was now working in the ministry of rites, I had to go and see him because there were rumours that my friend was fawning over the king to get a promotion, I was aware that his current position was considered inferior, his job was to stay at home and copy historical documents for the ministry of rites, I'd travelled on horseback all night long and made it to the capital by daybreak, my friend looked nervous when I showed up at his door without notice, he hurriedly hid his papers in a drawer as soon as he saw me, which caused me to suspect there was some unsound business going on, the sight of my old friend after a long period of separation filled me with deep frustration instead of joy, 'are you hiding something from me,' I asked, and noticed his lips were smeared with cuneiform signs, 'there's nothing to hide at all,' my friend stammered, I reached over and pulled out of his drawer all the documents he was hiding: a papyrus scroll full of cuneiform signs, a sheet of brown paper filled with Nôm characters, texts on the policies of the monarchs of ancient Egypt known as pharaohs, was he seriously learning how to turn himself into a king? the passing thought was enough to make my blood boil, without saying farewell, I quietly got on my horse and went home, perhaps it was true that those words and signs were going to propel him to a more desirable position, on my way back to the village, I couldn't stop thinking about him, my childhood friend.

* * *

Note:

accept my sincere apologies, please, Dr Lê Quân, it's only because i wished your text to appear more contemporary that i've taken the liberty to add a couple of additional words to your text.

35

in my village, there was another person, Mr Two the rice-mortar-binder, barely lettered when he was alive, but after his death, he transformed into a true intellectual and came back to the village with the sole mission to answer my inquiries, which were the inquiries of a naughty little child, at one point, when he'd completed what could be called an intellectual feat of the barefoot people, i blurted out a rather naive question: 'Mr Two, are you riding your rice mortar for fun?' as it turned out, Mr Two the rice-mortar-binder was trying out his device, in other words, he was testing the milling function of his rice mortar

'tell you what, young one, back then I had plenty of intelligence to answer your questions, but whenever I opened my mouth, I felt like I lacked the words to speak of an event for which even our ancestors might not have had the words to describe'

to my innocent mind back then, Mr Two the rice-mortar-binder was an extremely powerful man who had the nerve to bring back the termite mounds from a pagoda full of ghosts in order to make his rice mortars, he was the definition of a powerful man in my book, one day, although the rice mortar in our house hadn't expired yet, my father, a barefoot villager who liked to splurge, made up his mind over dinner and said to my mother, 'my wife, please go and find Mr Two the rice-mortar-binder,' the following dawn, the powerful rice-mortar-binder paid my father a visit, 'your grinder was made just a little over a year ago, how could it be already broken?' Mr Two asked, 'it's not yet broken, but the children's mother would like a new mortar for the family,' replied my father, and so a succinct contract was signed between my father, the extravagant barefoot man, and Mr Two, the powerful rice-mortar-binder

'you see, back then, i had to go everywhere by myself and take the job that no one else wanted to take, the weaving of the two covers for the mortar would take me many long hours, and so did the closing of its upper board, but it was the binding of the lower board that would take up an entire day, you see, seven generations of my family, my generation included, had perfected the craft of binding together the parts of a rice mortar, why do we say "binding" a rice mortar instead of simply "making" a rice mortar? do you know why that is? we say "binding" to emphasize the teeth of this device, to make the teeth, one has to bind these wooden pieces together and deploy them in the right formation, so that the mortar could perform its function, that is, the removal of the husk from the grain'

back then, i was so passionate about watching the binding of the rice mortars that i kept wishing the mortar in my house would break, so that i could see that powerful man again and watch him pour out of his old burlap sack his magical process, nowadays people often talk about the great process of industrialization and modernization, but i was enchanted by the unique process made possible by those marvellous tools that poured out of his old burlap sack, i remember clearly how they were all made of bamboo and wood, those palm-sized square pieces of wood, called the teeth of the mortar, were always sanded to a glistening finish, his mallets and chisels were all made of sturdy dried bamboo stumps, and whenever the mallet touched the chisel, the echoes that belonged to the fields would start to resound, then there was also the resilient clay of the termite mounds, stolen from the ghosts of the haunted pagoda, that was added to the mortar's cover, i often wondered if that was the moment Mr Two demonstrated his powerful existence to the world, i still remember the way he used the most forceful movements of his body to press the clay, which carried the scent of ghosts, upon the mortar's cover, then came the most decisive moment of the whole process, which was no less glorious than, excuse my flawed comparison, the assembling of a spacecraft today, when he gravely scattered the wooden teeth onto the clay that carried the scent of ghosts, immediately the wooden teeth deployed themselves in a battle formation, it seemed that his entire intellectual power was musically composed into this battle formation of the mortar's teeth, generating what appeared to be a superb harmony of classical mechanics, wouldn't the creation of a rice mortar rightfully belong to the field of classical mechanics? i use the word 'harmony' because as he was bending over with his mallets and chisels and beginning to press, slap and pound the clay, the infinite echoes of the fields started to resound with fervour, then finally he looked up, slightly swaying his body as if to shake off all the errors and imperfections from the great undertaking of adjusting the battle formation of the mortar's teeth

'right, i must tell you, back then i heard that in the west, unlike folks in our land, they wanted to make all their machines out of metal, i must say our ancestors were extraordinarily gifted to have devised a rice mortar entirely out of bamboo and wood'

and so that was how he returned to my village and fulfilled his sole mission to teach me about the rice mortar; there was another man known as Mr Lê Quí Đôn, whom i've previously mentioned, a reputed scholar in our country who became a mandarin in Phú Xuân and wrote *The Miscellaneous Chronicles of the Pacified Frontier*, in which he mentioned the land of Thuận Hóa, which encompassed my village, but he went into detail about only the crafts of weaving fabrics, weaving bamboo mats, making conical hats, casting pots and casting platters, he was a reputed scholar and

yet in the passage about ploughing, which was the main occupation
of the barefoot people in Thuận Hóa, he wrote down only a single
line, 'There was abundant rice throughout the three provinces of
Qui Nhơn, Quảng Ngãi and Gia Định,' without half a mention
of the rice mortar which was inseparable from the rice grains, and
then there was Mr Phan Huy Chú, also a national scholar, who
began in the early nineteenth century to compile an encyclopaedia
called *Regulations of Successive Dynasties by Subject Matter*, more
than a thousand pages long, and neither did he dedicate even half
a sentence to our rice mortar

'honestly, that day when you asked me whether i was riding the
rice mortar for fun, i was holding its crank to test a mortar i'd just
finished binding, but all the while i was dreaming of countries
like Java or India, to tell you the truth, i was always longing for a
silk robe, or a pair of lacquer silk trousers, yes, i was dreaming of
all kinds of plain silk and lacquer silk, and dreaming, too, of their
remote countries'

he'd only been dead for a few decades and yet his manner of speech
had drastically changed, whenever he spoke about the life of a rice
mortar, he always emphasized the role of its teeth and how they
managed to remove the husk of the grain, the existence of this
element depended on the existence of that element, it was the manner
of speech of a learned man, could it be that after his death, Mr Two
the rice-mortar-binder had transformed into a profound thinker?

'it's nothing, really, long before my time, the Chinese were said to
be the culprits behind our crisis, whereas during my time, it was
the Westerners who were said to be the culprits behind our crisis,
we barefoot people easily fell into crippling crises, doesn't matter,
really, you tell your children something, then your children tell it
to their children, here i am telling you my own theory, that our
ancestors had to be exceptionally gifted to have invented the rice

mortar, holding the mortar's crank and milling the rice, i felt like i was going somewhere very far, felt like i was going far and at the same time not moving at all, holding the mortar's crank and milling the rice, i realized i was at rest and at the same time, not at rest at all, as in i realized i was merely circling this worldly realm, and this sole realization that one was merely circling this worldly realm was enough to avoid the crippling paralysis of the brain'

well, let's just call him the father of this special branch of philosophy.

36

a suffering that reigns for a long time, or a gladness that crosses one's life, or an awakening that comes after months and years of blind passions, or a festive return of someone long dead . . . after all, wasn't my village a place where the trials of existence unfolded? thirty people, and not forty people as commonly believed, thirty people once went to the Upper Forest, the forested land that kept extending from the endlessness of the Mun Mountain, there weren't just the thirty of them but also verdant vegetation, creeks filled with mosquitoes and leeches, birds crying all day long, gentle animals like deer and hares, and hostile animals like elephants, bears and tigers, they were always fighting each other for a dwelling place, a struggle quiet and ruthless, everyday countless beings fell down, trees in the forest fell, wild animals fell, birds fell, humans fell, the venomous air of the mountain devoured the humans, the mosquitoes and leeches devoured the humans, the snakes, elephants and tigers devoured the humans, and the humans devoured the forests, devoured the birds, devoured the deer, hares and elephants, nobody knew for how many months and years this back-and-forth devouring lasted, in the end, among the people who went to the Upper Forest, someone was able to talk to the wild animals, nobody knew what this person said to the animals, in the end, the wild animals receded into the deep niches of the mountain, yielding the land of the Upper Forest to the humans, by the time the Tượng stream (which was the convergence of all

the streams that originated in the Mun Mountain, the stream that
flowed when it rained, and drained when it stopped raining) had
flowed through the land where rice and legumes were thriving,
it later came to be known as the Tượng river, and out of all the
people who first went to the Upper Forest, only three survived,
that was how the story had gone for hundreds of years, causing the
descendants in the village to relentlessly and sleeplessly wonder
whether or not their birthplace was an experimental community
for both rational beings like humans and irrational beings like
snakes, worms, birds, elephants or tigers, and whether it ultimately
turned out to be a failed experiment of creation, late one night
while i was pondering the book of village history i was writing,
'but do you have any idea how it all began?' Dr Quân (the late-
eighteenth-century Dr Lê Quân of my village) suddenly broke my
train of thought and made me wonder why Dr Quân, out of all
people, was paying me a visit, if the story he was about to tell
me were true, then my book of history might benefit from the
observation of a superb writer who had lived centuries ago, 'sir, this
descendant is listening,' i said, outside the nightjars had awoken
by the fences, a soft flap of their wings knocked on the night as if
engraving on the moving air the story of an uncommon encounter,
the flapping wings of the nightjars made a sound that was like a
gentle articulation of being, but Dr Quân's manner of speech was
more like a slowing down or a brief pause of a watercourse before
it resumed flowing again through a series of perilous turns

'in the beginning there was silence, wasn't there?' Dr Quân began
telling the story, 'but that couldn't be right, something must have
bred all the sounds and echoes that came afterwards, like the
deep roars of mountains, and the screams of humans on earth, or
could it be that in the beginning there was the greatest echo of all
echoes, but then what was it that bred all the silences afterwards,
for thousands of years the rocky cliffs have remained mute, and the
sky and earth have never said a thing, either, the earth and sky have
remained silent in the truest sense of the word, or could it be that in

the beginning there were both silences and echoes in the sky? but then which of them could explain all that happened afterwards? it was always either just this or just that, either eternal truths or great errors, one day in July, sunny day, the rice in the fields had turned dry after long rainless months, the fruit-bearing trees in my garden were waiting for rain like the rice in the fields, I thought the trees looked exhausted as though they'd gotten lost in a world devoid of connections between things, and yet there were some connections still, for instance, in the shade of the trees, the chickens were resting and hiding from the sun, although it certainly wasn't an adequate enough shelter for these miserable chickens whose only chance of survival depended on the few little insects left in the garden soil, these days, the changes in sunlight alone could wreak havoc on this tiny village, I kept feeling like there was someone, who could it be, someone smiling and watching us all, the withering rice in the fields, the thirsty plants and hungry chicken in the garden, and I myself who was powerless to manage the land, could someone be playing tricks on us, suddenly the old lady next door turned up at my door, crying for help, "please, you are the most learned person in the village, please save this old lady's son," the old lady gasped through her missing teeth, for some reason she assumed that my words could prevent the fury of history, I hurried over to her house, where a mortal soul was being hurled out of existence, a young man was shaking in a pool of blood, the one who had extinguished the young man's life was an enraged man whose fury showed on his face and in the way he held his sword

"'anyone who breaks the rule of the righteous must die,'" he shouted before he ordered his followers to leave the old lady's house, I knew that any human waving the flag of righteousness must have come from some historical alleyway where one could still consider oneself righteous, and how ironic that the old lady's son, the gentlest being in the village, was considered unrighteous by that ostensibly righteous human, ravens were gathering and crowding the sky above my head, were they bidding farewell to someone who had left this life, or was it simply due to the smell of blood, or due to the dying chickens in the gardens all over the village? the ravens, if they were gathering to prepare for a hunt, would also count as a flock of assassins, I, the most lettered person in the village, couldn't figure out how so much could happen in such a short time, later on, after I had died for a good while, I likewise couldn't figure out how this happened either, I ran into the bastard who had stabbed the old lady's son with his sword, he was now leading a group of terribly sad people the same way he'd done when he murdered the old lady's son, it turned out that sadness troubled the dead as much as the living, and when that bastard saw me, he had the same look of arrogance on his face that I'd seen before, now you, the scribe who record the history of the village, could you please tell me what any of this means, how could the human race only care about this thing called history . . .?'

it was an extremely confusing and entangled dream, upon waking up, i just lay in bed as i kept thinking about these words of Dr Quân in the dream.

37

finally, we managed to have a reunion, my parents, my big brother Lực and i,

'are you all right there?' noticing my brother's struggle to rearrange the bones of his arms and legs, my father asked,

meanwhile my mother simply sat there wiping her tears,

my brother had died before my parents did, he died twice, in fact: the first time, he was hung in the blood-soaked purge of the village; the second time, he was hit by a bomb in the cemetery knoll of the village,

'these goddamn bones torture me all the time, father,' my big brother Lực said, showing no sign of pain, but still i gave him some bandage to dress the wounds on his limbs,

it was a night in March, the insects by the fence in front of my house were starting their midnight serenade, i call it a serenade so that our reunion, which could only happen in the night, would sound more ceremonious,

'sad,' my father said, the sound of the insects along the fences made him sad, i told him they cried perpetually like that every single night, my mother went looking for her basket of betel leaves, 'let me get it for you, mother,' i offered, for more than thirty years i'd carefully kept my mother's betel basket in our wooden cabinet,

'have some tea before it gets cold,' i said to my father and brother, i'd made the tea as soon as the early evening wind delivered to me my father's message that tonight my parents and brother were going to come home,

'our reunion is like a once-in-a-century dream,' my big brother Lực said, slowly wobbling to the table to sip some tea,

'how's it going, son, how are you doing with the negotiation?' my father asked me,

'there's no negotiation yet, father, no encounter is allowed between the living and the dead, that is the latest doctrine that the state has popularized all over our land,' i replied, i knew my father had been spending all his energy on the question of how to maintain a dialogue he considered crucial for the existence of mankind, that is, the dialogue between the living and the dead, to him, in the precarious evolution of humankind, the conversations between the past and the present were matters of life and death, this time, compared to his previous returns, i noticed that my father seemed different, he looked saddened and troubled, was he trying to tell me something urgent before he could no longer see me ever again? it wasn't until almost dawn that he finally said it:

> I have passed through ninety-nine circles of hell, spoken the language of an exile, seen through the eyes of someone who left the world, I have left the world for a long while, and yet, still haunting my memory which I thought had already left me was the afternoon sound of a calf separated from its mother, and the sound of a nightjar flapping its wings as it tries to fly away

from the fences by the alleyway, these illusions, or these non-illusions, still haunt my memory which I thought had already left me, noon, I see someone tilt their face skyward and sing under the sun a song about a black snake sliding across the country, who could recount all the arbitrary exoduses of things, night, I see a breeze travel through the trees along the alleyway, one person goes, then one hundred thousand people go, for thousands of years now people have gone on the same quest, the world is an infinite quest, I have passed through ninety-nine empires of the dead, where there is neither the greatest nor the not-greatest, here among the dead I see ignorance and dogma stagger as if they had no refuge left, ignorance and dogma are still hiding in those literary books that never give humans any joy, and they too hide in the cruelty of human beings, here I am speaking of the empires of equality, the equality of death, I have passed through ninety-nine empires of equality, pretending to be the emperor of the empires and pretending to be the subject of the empires also, I had this dialogue with myself, 'your majesty, could the doctrine of death be the foundation for the existence of our empire?' 'there is no doctrine here, doctrine is merely a worldly language invented to console mortal humans in the smallness and brevity of their lives,' the emperor replied and gave me a stern look, alarmed, I tried touching my head, then tried touching my limbs, and felt as if warm blood was circulating in my body

i saw my father cry, for the first time ever since he died, i saw my father cry,

'and what about that village chief, is he alive or not?' my father suddenly turned to me and asked,

the morning crow of a rooster was already echoing from the other end of the village, 'whose rooster is crowing so loud?' my mother asked, her voice full of regret, she knew it was time to leave,

'well, i should get going,' my big brother Lực said, and hurriedly he sailed to the alleyway, by then many roosters were crowing all over the village, i knew my brother was afraid of having to see the earthly daylight again,

the village chief, the crook who took my father prisoner for his crime of reading day and night, died long ago, i only had enough time to relay that bit of village news to my father as he helped my mother stand up,

'what a pity that i can't bring the betel basket with me,' my mother said, wiping her tears as she looked at me,

'history is only a draft copy, son, nothing is certain, nothing is true,' my father reminded me before he took my mother's hand, and quietly they sailed to the alleyway.

Giã

8/2014–12/2017

Translator's Afterword

Soil and Scent

not admiration or victories
but simply to be accepted
as part of an undeniable Reality,
as stones and trees.

—Jorge Luis Borges

Chronicles of a Village is a web of tales woven around a nameless village where the narrator, also nameless, was born. This narrator, self-designated as the scribe who records village news, refers to himself using the lowercase, first-person, singular pronoun 'i'. His village is somewhere near the Mun Mountain in Central Vietnam, the region where the author, Nguyễn Thanh Hiện, was born. What unfolds in this little village at the foot of the Mun Mountain is a series of story fragments in which the author's autobiographical memories and fictions lyrically mingle. The tales reflect and refract the past and ongoing catastrophes of a land—dynastic crises, colonial policies, asphyxiating modernization. The pastoral harmony of the mountainside village is transformed, or deformed, by the years of war and indoctrination in the name of progress. By writing down the self-admittedly slippery, moth-eaten memories of his own and his fellow villagers', the scribe eternalizes the vanishing beauty of his village, page after page. He is the vessel through which the land, now barren, tells its myriad stories of sacred forests, fantastical animals, ordinary as well as mythical humans, all entangled in events now mundane, now wholly bizarre.

By calling his constellation of wandering tales a novel, Nguyễn Thanh Hiện disturbs the conventions of the plot-driven novel, not to mention the common rules of punctuation. He uses only commas instead of periods to mark the breaks between sentences, which creates the effect of the narrator speaking in one long breath, with small pauses in between instead of full stops. The news and dialogues recorded by the scribe, often seemingly random or unfinished, suggest that not only the construction of the sentence but our idea of history also turns out to be a fiction, and thus can be prolonged and reshaped. Similar to how a riverine sentence or a tortuous thought can go on for as long as entire pages, history in Nguyễn Thanh Hiện's conception also embodies a sense of ceaselessness, shifting with each teller, each gaze. It is this perpetual shape-shifting quality that makes the stories so unpredictably mesmerizing.

The magic of Nguyễn Thanh Hiện's work lies in the oral quality of his written words. Orality shimmers, for example, in the way the narrator's father describes a mythical birdsong as a tune he heard from his father, who heard it from his father, who must have also heard it from his father, and so on. It shines, too, in the narrator's memory of his mother singing him lullabies about animals frolicking on a distant, cloud-swathed mountaintop. Orality also shapes the way a radio broadcast can be transmitted through the village by word of mouth and reinvented into comical mistranslations. The sound of these soaring pieces of news, lullabies and birdsongs, instead of the memory of written books, is what most persistently haunts the narrator. He also frequently recalls the vivid sense of oneness that he once felt as a child, back when humans, nature and ancient folk myths lived together in fairy-tale harmony. The genealogies and cryptic dreams that he records carry the vagaries of time as they shift with each teller who relayed their stories to him. The things heard and retold by the scribe—tales of avaricious French colonists, stories of ill-starred humans reincarnating as birds, reports on recent land-grabbers and other cruel games of history—all have a nonchalant sense of incompleteness about them. These protean tales, which are disorderly, personal, repetitive and subject to the revisions of each speaker, articulate the ungraspable and changeful face of history: peace in our earthly realm is impermanent; disasters might break out any time; thriving dynasties could suddenly collapse overnight, and the heroes of yesterday are suddenly labelled traitors; the winners and losers of history are always being rewritten without end.

The interwoven stories in this book can thus sound both historical and fictive, written and oral, colloquial and solemn, thereby challenging the usual legible mood and forward motion of the Western novel. With his deliberate lack of full stops and capitalization, Nguyễn Thanh Hiện writes down his perception of history in a manner akin to what he calls an act of drifting. To write is to drift, as he once said. Writing is a way for the wandering bard to record how he drifts in the world and notes down the things he sees. The spontaneity of this drifting method unleashes him from the confines of bookish reason and ossified sources of official history. Among his stories of war, revolution and later on, new breeds of civilized, lettered and financially savvy humans, there are many tales that, instead of attempting comprehensive sketches of Vietnam, centre intimate relations or peculiar events, like the scribe's memories of his father who carried the plough while exhaling poetry, or the memory of a wounded, bloody mountain crying out for help. The digressive tales and details, both historical and mythopoetic, portray a land that is at once cosmic and quotidian, idyllic and vulnerable to turbulent changes. It is a land made up of splendid forests and creeks as well as scenes of ecological destruction, charming love stories as well as sweeping collective catastrophes. Anchored by contemporary phenomena that blend with ancestral knowledge, the tales spoken or sung by the scribe feels both timely and timeless.

One of Nguyễn Thanh Hiện's timely and timeless phrases that occurs throughout the stories is 'rice and fabric' (cơm áo), whose English equivalent could be 'bread', 'livelihood' or 'means of subsistence'. When the narrator speaks of 'rice and fabric worries', he is referring to the perennial struggle of the peasant to make ends meet, or as the Vietnamese say, to take care of rice and fabric matters. A decent harvest and a couple robes to wear are the dreams of every farming household—humble dreams easily crushed by a sudden change in weather. Quiet worries about rice, clothes and the weather's disastrous fickleness run in the village like a weary rhythm from one generation to another, cancelling the possibilities of romanticizing rural hardship. Yet despite this rhythm of poverty, hunger and toil, the scribe's father, a ploughman-poet, kept nurturing his profound love for a life attached to the soil, sky, rain and sun. He found the way that the earth yields rice and cotton to be astoundingly elegant, calling the emergence of a new sprout 'the song of soil', an exquisite musical movement that nourishes our being. The ploughman-poet, under no illusion about rural life, dwells in the forgotten elegance of ploughing the fields, walking with the cows, entering the rhythm of earth and sky.

Birthsoil is another imagery that recurs in the scribe's meditations. Birthsoil is my way of translating the Vietnamese word quê, usually translated as 'homeland' or 'hometown'. Birthsoil summons the image of soil as a space of creation, the burial ground of one's placenta and umbilical cord, the base of one's existence and nourishment. The soil of the village bears the seeds of the cotton and rice plants that sustain the scribe's family. It also bears the roots of the banana grove that witnessed his nervous teenage attempt to strike up a conversation with a girl in the village. The same soil bears, too, the impact of war bombs that took away the lives of his loved ones. 'My village' is a dumpy couple of words that bring to his mind all kinds of memory linked to his birthsoil, from the fatigue of the industrious adults to the fleeting romance of his youthful years, from the sighs of grandmothers humming at noon to the delightful cries of little cowherds playing in the forest. One's love for the land runs in the body like a divine flow of rice wine, as declared by Mr Hoành, an elder in the village whose homemade wine distils the purest flavours of heaven and earth. The intoxicating fragrances of the land run on and on in the memory of the villagers to whom their birthsoil is deathless because remembered.

Over the years, war bombs, political purges and various other forms of suffocation have triggered countless cycles of persecution and death in the village. In an era when humans are mostly invested in the growth and futural profit of the living, the scribe tells us tales that resist the lethal, progress-driven impulse to forget the dead. His dreamlike stories recall the vanished cries of the night herons, the young cowherds shot dead in the crossfire of war, the villagers who died unjust deaths. They are grief-honouring tales that will 'not allow the dead to be killed', as said by Zbignew Herbert. It is in the night, the time of resting, reminiscing and dreaming, that the scribe often descends into his flickering pool of memory, a zone ridden with ghosts of times past. In the night, the smiles and cries of his long-gone ancestors, family and fellow villagers often return to the soil of his mind, along with 'many voices of leaves, of birds, of rocks, of streams sinking into the flow of time.' The scribe is a human who remembers the traces of the dead, whose sorrow and wisdom flood the pages of his village history.

My translation is an attempt to listen to, while recreating, the scribe-narrator's rhythm of spoken eloquence, nostalgia and contemplation—an entrancing rhythm embedded in the dignified simplicity of the original Vietnamese. A translator is someone trying to grasp not only the rhythm or tone, but the scent of the text. It so happens that in Vietnamese, the noun *hương* (rooted in the character 香), meaning 'scent' or 'perfume', is homonymous with another noun *hương*, rooted in 鄉, meaning 'village', 'native land' or, as I often say, 'birthsoil'. As the sound of *hương* recurs in *Chronicles*, these two homonyms have woven in my mind a tapestry of birthsoil memories, redolent with the aromatic traces that wind their way through the village roads: the scent of ripe mangoes, the scent of pomelo flowers, the scent of rain, the scent of mountain ghosts, the scent of upturned soil, the scent of young rice, the scent of grass. These fragrances of nature are the magical moments of reverie that float between the scribe and the bedlam of the world. His remarkable store of memories is infused with scents so sharp and inextinguishable that they have at times absorbed my translation into their perfumed cosmos. If you peer closely at the pages, perhaps you too can feel the traces of this persistent perfume which flies beyond language. A blend of the wild odours of the forest, the earthy aroma of childhood playtime, the giddy fragrance of adolescent adventures and also the familiar blood-smudged smell of war and venomous ideology, the scent of the village is an ephemeral, indelible medium through which the ancestral land remembers its vanished woods, its forgotten meadows, its drifting chroniclers. The memory of the land is a thousand sweetbitter fragrances gathered into an endlessness that floats in the sky of your mind.

Quyên Nguyễn-Hoàng

Acknowledgements

The translator would like to thank: Nguyễn Thanh Hiện, Tu McAmmond, Nguyễn Lâm Thảo Thi, the PEN/Heim Translation Fund, Bill Johnston, Izzah Farzanah Ahmad, Nicole Wong, Trương Công Tùng, and most of all, Nhã Thuyên, Kaitlin Rees, Chenxing Han, Trent Walker and Anh Thèo. Grateful acknowledgement is made to the editors and publishers of magazines in which the translations of some chapters in this book first appeared: the *Margins* (the *Asian American Writers' Workshop*): Chapter 15, and *Lunch Ticket Magazine*: Chapters 1, 5, 12 and 14.

Nguyễn Thanh Hiện was born in 1940 in Nam Tượng village, An Nhơn district, Bình Định Province in Vietnam, the country central to his literary works.

He graduated with a BA in Western philosophy from the Saigon University of Literature. During the Vietnam War, he participated in the student movement against the war in Saigon and wrote stories for the anti-war magazines *Trình Bày* and *Đối Diện*. Currently he is based in Qui Nhơn city, vernacularly known as Giã, where he works as an educator and author.

He has written twenty-four novels, twenty-two epic poems, three volumes of short stories and numerous poems, some of which have been printed into books and a variety of which have been widely published on domestic and foreign literary websites.

Quyên Nguyễn-Hoàng is a writer, translator and art curator born in Vietnam. Her poems and translations have appeared on *Poetry* Magazine, *Jacket2*, the *Margins*, and various literary anthologies and exhibition catalogues. She is a Stanford University graduate, a 2020 PEN/Heim Translation grant recipient and a winner of the Winter/Spring 2022 Gabo Prize for Literature in Translation.